A Portrait of Love

A PORTRAIT OF LOVE

W.E.D. Ross

AVALON BOOKS
THOMAS BOUREGY AND COMPANY, INC.
NEW YORK

PRINTED IN THE UNITED STATES OF AMERICA
BY HADDON CRAFTSMEN, SCRANTON, PENNSYLVANIA

To my good friend Marion Wait, Kennel Club judge and
executive officer of the Animal Rescue League

CHAPTER ONE

From the moment Sally Sheldon's plane had landed in Holland, she had been enchanted. Winning a month's trip to Amsterdam, with all expenses paid, had been like an exciting dream come true.

Now she was on the third morning of her visit, and the June weather was sunny and perfect. The airline had placed her in a small hotel not far from the heart of the city. She'd already taken a couple of walks to acquaint herself with the winding streets, the fine old buildings, and the many canals.

Almost everyone spoke English to some degree, many perfectly. That made it easy for

1

Sally to get around. She found the Dutch people pleasant and was amazed at how many of them, young and old, traveled around the city on bicycles.

Walking briskly, Sally still thought it incredible that she'd won this trip from an airline simply by sending them a completed crossword puzzle and proof that she'd traveled with them in the past.

She paused before the window of a jewelry store, checking her appearance. Her short, curly dark hair was in order, and her beige pantsuit complemented it nicely. Sally walked on, keeping her blue-gray eyes wide open for sights of interest.

Ahead of her was the square with the war memorial. The Royal Palace was across the street. And nearby a puppeteer was putting on a comedy show. He worked behind his small stage, manipulating the movement of the puppets and dubbing in their voices. An appreciative crowd had gathered to watch him.

Just a short distance away from the crowd, a tall young man with an easel was painting the war memorial. Sally moved away from the puppet show to observe the artist. He had great skill and worked with quick strokes.

As he paused to change his paintbrush, she said, "I hope you understand English. I think you're extremely talented."

He turned to offer her a smile, looking rather

handsome with his blond hair and blue eyes. He was probably about twenty-seven and wore blue jeans and a checkered red-and-white shirt open at the neck.

"You speak like an American," he told her, continuing with his work.

She stared at him. "And you also sound like one."

The young man laughed easily. "I happen to be from the States. New York City to be exact."

Sally gasped. "I can't believe it! So do I!"

"So we had to come to Amsterdam to meet," he said. "But that isn't so strange. Where in the city do you live and work?"

"I work up on Park Avenue," she said. "I'm a secretary in a law office. And I live with two girlfriends in the East Eighties."

He shook his head. "No wonder we've never met. I live in the East Village and have my studio there. I hardly ever go uptown." He extended his hand. "My name is Adam Bond."

Sally put her small hand in his large one. "I'm Sally Sheldon," she said, feeling suddenly shy.

His eyes twinkling, he said, "I don't often mix with tourists, but it's a pleasure to meet you."

"I'm glad," she replied. "I'm not anxious to spend my time here with tourists either."

"But you are one!"

"Not in the strict sense."

He said, "I'm not certain I get your meaning."

Sally laughed. "I'm not a tourist in the sense that I planned to come here. I won a contest conducted by an airline. The prize happened to be a month with all expenses paid in Mexico City or Amsterdam. I chose Amsterdam."

"You made a wise choice," Adam Bond said. "I visited Mexico City once and it is interesting, but my personal preference is for Amsterdam."

"Are you living here permanently?"

He shook his head. "No. I came over for a year of work and study. I'm actually a portrait artist. I've done several since I've been here. One of them an important commission which will pay the balance of my expenses here and give me a start again in New York."

Sally said, "I think being an artist is wonderful. It gives you such freedom."

Adam looked rueful. "We have freedom, no question of that. But if we're not lucky, it can be a freedom to starve."

She studied his painting. "If all your work is that good, I'd think you'd have no trouble selling it."

"Thanks," he said. "I'm always in need of encouragement." He glanced at the canvas. "I can't do anything more with this now."

"You'll take it to your studio?"

He nodded and dismantled the easel. "You

haven't been here long, have you?"

"My third day," Sally said happily. "I've had a grand time walking around."

"And almost the whole month still ahead of you," he said, adjusting his painting and folded easel under his arms. "My studio is only a short distance away. I have a lot of my stuff there. Would you like to see it?"

It was an invitation from a stranger in a strange city, but Sally was so impressed by him she decided to accept. "I'd like that," she said. "You're the first friend I've made since getting here, unless you count the elevator man at the hotel."

He moved away from the bustle of the square. "I don't know too many people," he admitted. "But I can introduce you to a few."

"I'm still numbed with the wonder of it all," she said. "I doubt that I'd ever have seen Amsterdam if I hadn't won that contest."

"I know," he said. "Pay is good in New York, but your expenses must be high. Especially if you live in Manhattan."

"You can say that again. But it's such an exciting city. I don't think I'd want to live anywhere else at the moment."

"You had no trouble getting a month's vacation?"

"My boss was very good about it," she said. "He arranged it all with the firm. He didn't want me to miss this chance."

"Very decent of him," Adam Bond said. "But

wasn't there a boyfriend to object to your being away so long or who would want to join you here?"

Sally felt her cheeks warm. "By a strange twist of fate, the boyfriend I had was transferred to California a few months ago, and he hasn't even written me since. So I didn't bother letting him know."

"Very wise," the young artist said.

They were walking down a narrow old street now.

Adam stopped when they came to a green door in a two-story brick building. "My studio is upstairs."

He unlocked the front door and she followed him up a steep flight of stairs to a dark hallway. Soon he led Sally into a large, white-walled room with an impressive skylight. All around on the walls were his paintings, and on a large easel directly under the skylight was a huge unfinished portrait of an interesting-looking elderly woman.

Sally glanced around her. "It's just what I expected. Perfect for a studio."

Adam put down the easel and painting he was carrying. "I'm glad you approve," he said. "I spent some time finding this place. I have a kitchen and a bedroom in the back. I'll make us some coffee while you look around." And he left her to vanish through a door at the rear of the big room.

"Thanks!" she called after him.

Then she eagerly began making the rounds of the various oils and watercolors. The watercolors included a handsome study of a windmill, an old church, and a canal. They were charming. Some of the oils also depicted attractive city and country scenes.

But it was the display of portraits that most showed Adam's talent. His studies of various children and adults were fascinating. There was one especially fine painting of a beautiful young woman with auburn hair and almond-shaped green eyes under a high forehead. With deceptive simplicity, the portrait showed her to be intelligent, intense, and perhaps a touch haughty.

Sally's last stop was the big unfinished portrait of the old woman. She had a strong face, a stern mouth. It was the sort of face that had probably never been beautiful but would always be striking.

Sally was still standing before the big easel when Adam Bond came back carrying a tray with cups, a coffeepot, and a plate of cookies. He placed them on a round table and beckoned her to join him.

She came over and said, "I think your work is wonderful. The portrait you're doing now could be a masterpiece."

He smiled in appreciation. "I hope you're right," he said. "I've spent a long while on it.

Now it's almost done. I'm counting on my fee for it to pay up my debts and get me back to New York."

Sally sat down and poured some coffee for them. "The woman has a strong face and she looks as if she might be wealthy."

"Heaps of money," he said. "One of the few remaining old New York aristocrats. Made all their money in mining years ago."

"How interesting," Sally said. "She's a lucky woman."

He helped himself to a cookie and sipped his coffee. "I'm not so sure. I don't envy her the sort of life-style she has. For one thing, she's always fearful that people value her for her money rather than herself."

Sally glanced toward the painting. "You can almost see that," she said. "Who is she?"

"Vivian Lane," he said. "Name mean anything to you?"

"I'm afraid not."

"I'm not surprised. She's kept a low profile. Mixed up in a lot of philanthropies, but her photo and name seldom appear in the papers. She doesn't want that kind of publicity."

"I think I can understand," Sally said, then turned to the painting of the auburn-haired girl. "I found that one the next most interesting."

"Really?" A kind of reserved look crossed his handsome face. "Do you think she's beautiful?"

"I do," she said. "In a rather startling way. She has the look of someone with great determination, very intense, someone used to having things just as she wants them."

Adam looked pleased. He ran a hand through his mane of yellow hair. "Not bad! Did I get all that into the portrait?"

"All I know about her is what I see in your painting."

He leaned across the table and said very seriously, "You have just given me a great compliment. You've read her character very well."

"Who is she?"

He looked somewhat embarrassed. "You'll be surprised when I tell you. She's the niece and heir of Vivian Lane. Her name is Dorothy Lane. I met her in the square and decided to do a portrait of her."

Sally gave him a long look. "Dear me! You seem to make a practice of picking up young women in the square."

Adam raised a protesting hand. "Don't get that idea in your head! I knew Dorothy before I came over here. I met her at a Village party. She had stage ambitions for a while and had met several of my actor friends."

"Did she give up her stage ambitions?"

"I think so," the young artist said. "You never can be sure of anything with Dorothy. As you said, she's very strong-minded."

"And wealthy."

He nodded. "She lives near her aunt. Her parents are dead. It was through Dorothy I eventually managed to get the commission to do her aunt."

"How convenient," Sally said.

"Now wait a minute. Don't sell me short. It was my talent, not my charm, that really got me the commission. Vivian Lane had wanted a portrait done for a long time, and when she saw my study of Dorothy, she decided to hire me to do her."

"Well, it was fortunate the way it all turned out," Sally said.

"Yes, it was." He quickly poured himself some more coffee.

"Have they been in Amsterdam long?" she asked.

"Several months," he said. "The old woman has arthritis. She dotes on a doctor here. Says he's the only specialist who has ever helped her. So she comes here every year. She also has some old sentimental attachment to the place."

"With her money, she can choose a doctor anywhere," Sally said.

"Exactly," Adam Bond agreed. "And the man is famous. Much has been written about him all over the world."

"What about you?" she asked. "What made you decide to study art in Amsterdam rather than in Paris or Rome, even London?"

He got up and stood leaning against the

windowsill as he glanced out at the street. "I'd
been here before. I love the city and the country. In fact, my roots are here. My parents
came from Holland originally."

"And are they in New York now?"

He sighed. "No. They were killed in a car
crash three years ago."

"I'm sorry," Sally said. "You must miss
them."

"They were wonderful people. Both of them.
But it doesn't hurt as much as it used to."

She stood up and joined him at the window,
filled with sympathy. "Then you have no one?"

"Oh, I'm not completely alone in the world.
I have a few cousins and aunts and uncles.
And most importantly Uncle Theo. My moth-
er's brother."

"I'm so glad," she said with a rush of sincerity.

"He lives and works here in Amsterdam,"
Adam said. "That was another reason for my
wanting to return here."

"I should think it would be," she said. "What
does he do?"

"He's a diamond cutter," Adam said. "That's
a big industry here, you know."

"I know. This city seems to be filled with
industries and commerce. And plenty of art,
too."

"Speaking of commerce and art, sometimes
I think I should be a commercial artist, maybe
work in advertising. Give up the serious stuff."

"Why can't you do both?"

"That's what my uncle says." Adam paused. "I'd like to have you meet him."

"I'd be honored," she said.

"He enjoys meeting Americans and talking to them. Maybe I'll have Uncle Theo and you here for dinner one evening," Adam went on. "He's very young in his viewpoint. I know you'd get along with him."

"It's something I'll look forward to," she said.

"You will be here almost a month?"

"Yes. Only three days have gone by so far. I hope to go out and see the countryside. And maybe make a short trip to London. That will be at my own expense."

"Have you been there before?"

"No."

"Then it will be worthwhile," Adam said.

"I'm glad you feel that way," she said. "I wouldn't want to travel all the way over here without visiting London."

At that moment, the door to the studio was opened, and a young woman in a smart white suit came rushing in. It was the girl whose portrait Adam had painted, Dorothy Lane. She was even more beautiful in person than in the portrait.

Staring at Adam and Sally, she said rather coldly, "If I'm interrupting anything, I'll gladly leave."

CHAPTER TWO

Adam gasped, "Dorothy!" He took a step toward the girl.

Dorothy's green eyes were gleaming with annoyance. "You were supposed to meet me at the boutique a half hour ago!"

"Sorry," Adam said. "I didn't realize it was so late."

The auburn-haired girl now focused on Sally with a sour smile on her attractive face. "Obviously!"

"I just met Sally," he said. "She's visiting here from New York. I wanted her to see the studio."

Dorothy nodded. "I gathered that."

Sally tried to defuse the awkward situation. She walked over to the other girl and extended her hand. "My name is Sally Sheldon and I'm on vacation here for a month. I won a contest."

Dorothy limply shook her hand. "How fortunate."

Adam explained, "She won a prize offered by an airline, a month in Amsterdam with all expenses paid."

"Interesting," the auburn-haired girl said with a glacial smile. "And your entertaining her is a sort of extra?"

"We met in the square a little while ago. I wanted to see the studio," Sally said. "I'm sorry I made Adam late for his appointment with you."

For the first time Dorothy showed signs of relenting. "It's all right. I don't blame you in any case."

"Quite right," Adam said. "You know I have no sense of time. I was the one in the wrong. I'm ready to admit it."

"You always are," Dorothy said. Then she turned to Sally. "So you're to be here for a month?"

"Less three days."

Dorothy Lane stared at her in awe. "My, we are precise! You know I never had that sort of computer mind. I envy you, my dear. So you live in New York?"

"Yes."

"Let me guess," the girl said. "In the Bronx

or perhaps Staten Island?"

"I share an apartment in the East Eighties in Manhattan," Sally said, trying to keep her temper under control.

It was very clear Dorothy would not be among Adam's friends welcoming her to Amsterdam.

"A lot of working girls do that," Dorothy said with a hint of a sniff. "I could never stand any such arrangement. I like my privacy too much."

"But then you would never have to do anything like that," Sally said.

"No." The auburn-haired girl smiled. "Happily, I wouldn't."

Adam sounded casual as he told Dorothy, "We must have a party and see that Sally meets all our friends."

"Indeed," the other girl said, looking none too pleased. "It should be fun. With her mathematical mind, she'll count them off and give them all numbers."

Adam turned to Sally. "Dorothy enjoys making little jokes. She's famous for them."

"You're too generous, darling," the auburn-haired girl told him. "It's just that when facing difficult moments, I try to laugh."

Sally said, "I really must leave now. Adam, I like your studio and I think your paintings are excellent."

"I'll be in touch with you," he promised. "Where are you staying?"

"The Bergen House. It's a very small hotel, so there are no phones in the rooms. You could leave a message at the desk."

"Or phone someone in the house next door," Dorothy said sarcastically. "Tell me, Sally, are you a native New Yorker?"

"No. I come from a small town in Iowa."

"Really?" Dorothy said. "I've driven through Iowa. Vast place with more cows than people if I remember rightly."

"You rarely remember anything rightly," Adam told her.

Sally said, "We do have a lot of cows out there. In fact, my father is a dairy farmer."

"Which I suppose makes you a milkmaid," Dorothy said with a smile. "I gather that's where you became so adept at mathematics, counting all those cows."

"Cows have wonderful natures," Sally told her. "I like them a lot better than many people I've met since." She walked out of the studio with Adam behind her.

Adam escorted her down the stairway to the front door of the house. He said, "I must apologize for Dorothy. She's not always so hostile. She can be wonderful at times. But she's upset because I entirely forgot I was supposed to meet her."

Sally smiled. "My impression is that she blames me."

"It wasn't your fault, not anyone's fault," he protested. "The truth of it is she didn't make my meeting her at the boutique definite enough. It was a maybe thing."

"I hope her finding me in your studio doesn't make things worse for you."

He smiled. "Hey, I'm a free man. I'm not engaged to Dorothy or anything. We're just friends. Nothing more."

"Maybe she'd like there to be something more," Sally suggested.

The young artist glanced upstairs in the direction of the studio. "It's hard to read what is in her mind. We have been good friends, but I've never shown any jealousy over her other male friends. So why should she be so upset about you?"

She laughed softly. "I'm afraid I can't answer that." And she walked outside.

Adam followed her a couple of steps. "I do want to see you again. Please believe that."

Sally stopped. "It was fun. But you needn't feel you have to follow up in any way. I'm having a grand time exploring Amsterdam on my own."

"I'll be in touch soon," he said. "Not for your sake but for mine. I've enjoyed meeting you." And with a farewell smile, he waved to her. Then he went inside.

Walking back to the square, Sally found herself thinking of Adam. The time spent with him had been most pleasant until Dorothy had arrived. One thing seemed clear. Dorothy's interest in Adam was more than friendly

whether he realized it or not. And maybe sub-
consciously he was more interested in Dorothy
than he claimed to be. Wasn't that just like a
man?

Sally stopped to wait for a traffic light. The
great Gothic church on the nearest corner
looked very old but had clearly been recently
repaired. The light changed and she hurried
across the street. After a few minutes she was
in the square once again, in sight of the Royal
Palace. From there to her hotel was an easy
walk.

Feeling hunger, Sally stopped at a small
restaurant near the Bergen House. It was plain
in decor, and the food was neither fancy nor
expensive. But it was tasty enough. Sally
thought about Adam and Dorothy as she ate
and, with a small smile, pictured them in some
elegant restaurant.

Dorothy lived in an elegant, expensive world
and apparently had the idea of marrying Adam
Bond and taking him with her to the rare
heights of New York society. Sally was sure
of it. But she wasn't so sure of Adam's true
thoughts and feelings. Men claimed that
women were unpredictable and mysterious,
she mused, sighing. The exact opposite was
true. There was no greater enigma in the uni-
verse than the heart or mind of a man.

CHAPTER THREE

After lunch Sally returned to the hotel. The smiling, chubby elevator man greeted her like an old friend. She already knew his name was Jacob Schok. She was his sole passenger now in the tiny elevator.

"Are you seeing anything in Amsterdam?" the white-haired man wanted to know.

Sally smiled. "I'm gradually getting around. Especially to the spots near here."

"You must not miss the art gallery with the Rembrandts," he said.

"I've been there," she said. "On my first day."

"Good," he said, bringing the elevator to a halt. And with a wink, he advised, "And visit our great department store. Don't forget now."

"I mean to go there," she said.

"And the Historical Museum," he went on. "And the theaters and concerts. You must see everything you can."

"I'll do my best," she laughed. "I have almost a month left."

He nodded. "You will see plenty. But so many come here and see nothing. So interested in food or drink or business they have no time for the old city. It is a shame." He let her out.

Sally rested for a while, then wrote some cards to friends back in New York. She was just pasting a stamp on the last card when there was a knock on her door. Opening it, she found the elevator man, Jacob Schok, standing there.

He bowed in an old-fashioned way and said, "There is a gentleman downstairs asking to see you, Miss Sheldon."

She assumed it was Adam, since he was the only man she'd met since arriving in Amsterdam. Sally was surprised that he had turned up so soon but decided that she would see him.

"I'll be right down," she told Jacob Schok. "Let me get my things and fix my face." She did that quickly, then followed him to the elevator.

When Sally stepped out of the elevator, it was not Adam Bond she saw but an even taller young man with brown hair and a camera slung over his shoulder.

His smile was warm as he asked, "Are you the Sally Sheldon who won the Global Airlines contest?"

She nodded. "Yes. Are you from the airline?"

"Well, yes," he said. "I'm doing an assignment for their public relations department. We want to do a story on you. It will appear in some of our travel brochures and that sort of thing. The airline would like you to cooperate since the publicity helps them."

Taken by surprise, she hesitated. "No one said anything about this."

With another smile he took out his wallet and opened it and held it out for her to see. "This is my card, which proves I'm Frank Kincaide from the public relations department of Global Airlines."

Sally carefully read the card and saw that it bore out what he had said. She shrugged and asked, "What exactly are you planning on doing?"

"Something about you," he said, restoring the wallet to his pocket. "Plus your feelings about winning the contest. And your impressions of things over here. You see, I'm also doing a magazine article about the Americans in Amsterdam. I'd like to include you."

She gave him an amused look. "That sounds like a rather long assignment."

"I don't expect to do it in twenty minutes or even at one session," he said. "This is a fairly good magazine assignment. I want to do the

best job I can on it. For both the magazine and
the brochures."

"When do you wish to begin?"

"That depends on you."

She thought. "I suppose I'd like to get it over
and done with as soon as possible. We can start
right away if you like."

His lean, intelligent face brightened.
"Great!" he said. "I can't ask for more coop-
eration than that. Suppose we go somewhere
where we can sit comfortably and talk?"

"I'd ask you up to my room," she said. "But
it's small and dark."

"No. I know the exact place to begin. There's
a new Japanese hotel. A tall one. It has a cafe
in the penthouse with a wonderful view of the
city. We can have coffee, enjoy the view, and
get the interviews started."

"Is it far from here?" she wondered.

"We'll take a cab," he said, guiding her out
of the lobby. "Don't worry about the expense.
It all goes to Global Airlines. They give me a
generous allowance."

Sally smiled when they were in the cab.
"This is my lucky day. I'm to get a free sight-
seeing tour."

"I'll do my best," he said, giving her a keen
glance. "You know you don't look much like
the picture the airline gave me."

"No?"

"Not at all," he said. "You're much more
attractive."

"Thank you," she said, blushing. "But I'm willing to help you with your story without being flattered."

"It's not flattery," the young writer said. "Sober truth! I'm glad someone pretty like you won the contest. It will make the photographs more appealing."

Sally asked him, "How long have you been a writer?"

"About eight years," he said. "I've been in Europe three years doing travel articles and PR work. First in London, Denmark, Paris, Germany, Rome, Sweden, and now over here. I've been in this area for more than six months."

"Being a writer must be an exciting life," she said, studying his handsome profile.

"I like it," he said. "It's not for everyone. The girl I was engaged to marry gave me a choice. Give up being a travel writer or give her up."

"And?" she asked.

He smiled bleakly. "I'm still gadding about, doing travel pieces, and my girl is married to someone else. She didn't lose much time."

"Maybe it was for the best."

"I try to tell myself that," the young man said frankly. "But it was a blow to my pride."

"I had something of the same sort happen to me," she said, glancing out the taxi window at a street of low red-brick buildings.

"You did?" he sounded interested.

"Yes. The guy I was dating was transferred to the West Coast. He promised to write me as soon as he was settled. I haven't heard from him yet. That was some time ago."

"I get it," Frank Kincaide said. "He must have met one of the more interesting natives out there. Well, I can only sympathize by saying what you just told me: Maybe it was for the best."

"Right! But it's harder when I'm the one I'm trying to convince."

"I know," Frank said as the taxi came to a halt in front of a very modern hotel.

When they had taken the elevator to the penthouse cafe, the Japanese headwaiter showed them to a table for two right by the windows, with a breathtaking view of the city.

Impressed, Sally told Frank, "You know how to get good service."

He winked at her and said, "A generous tip from Global Airlines helped. The headwaiter happened to remember me from another visit."

"So you have interviewed many people up here?"

"A few," he said. "Not many. And no one like you. If you don't mind, I'm going to take your photo now. I'd like a few shots of you gazing out the window at the city below. Do you mind?"

She smiled. "Go ahead."

He carefully placed her at the best angle for the photos and then moved a little distance away and took several shots of her.

Returning to sit opposite her, he said, "I'm sure to have gotten at least one good one."

"I hope so," Sally said. "After all your trouble bringing me here."

"You were a secretary with a law firm, weren't you?"

"I still am," she told him. "They gave me a month's leave of absence. You've done your homework well."

"Give the credit to the Global PR office in New York. They wired me all the main details about you."

"You probably know a lot more about me than I do about you," she told him.

Frank Kincaide laughed. "Well, let me even up with you. I was born in Maine. Studied journalism in college, came to New York and got my first job at Metro Magazine in production. And I've been doing travel writing and PR work the last three years."

It was her turn to laugh. "That was a quick fill-in."

"From the cradle to the present," he said. "Now let's get down to some routine question stuff."

Which he did. But she noticed that he seemed interested in everything she said. It did not seem routine at all.

The session went on for an hour. Then Frank sat back and put his notebook in an inside pocket of his jacket. "That's enough for today."

"The time has passed so quickly," she said.

"I'm glad you feel that way," he told her. "Now tomorrow I'd like to take you to a small factory where you can watch wooden shoes being made. We'll do some photos and get one of you holding a shoe."

She laughed. "The folks back home should love it."

"That's the idea," he said. "Providing you can make time for me tomorrow."

"I'd like to have the morning to myself," she said. "Would the afternoon do? Right after lunch?"

He nodded. "Yes. Except Global Airlines buys your lunch. I'll find an interesting spot. Meet you at your hotel about twelve-thirty."

"That sounds lovely," she said.

"Now I'll get you home in a cab," he told her. "It's been quite a while since I've talked with an American girl as pretty as you. I don't suppose you're free for dinner tonight?"

Sally liked the young writer but didn't want to rush things too much. So she said, "Thanks for the invitation. I'll look forward to lunch tomorrow, but I'd prefer not to accept for tonight."

"Just as you say," he told her.

Downstairs, he found her a cab, paid the driver, and gave him the address of the Bergen House. Then he leaned in her window and said, "I'll be in your hotel lobby at twelve-thirty sharp."

"I'll be expecting you," she said.

And during the drive back to the hotel, Sally thought about it all. Within one day she had met two interesting young men. She had liked them both. It was too bad that Adam Bond was more or less spoken for.

When she entered the lobby of the small hotel, a buxom female clerk greeted her with a smile.

The woman pushed forward a vase filled with red roses and said, "These are for you."

Sally stared at the flowers. "There has to be a mistake!"

"No mistake," the clerk said. "A young man brought them here for you and left his card." She gave the girl a small envelope.

Sally hastily tore the envelope open and read its message.

"Hope you enjoy these. Would like to entertain you at dinner tonight. Will call for you at seven—Adam Bond."

As Sally stared at the card for a long moment, a smile crossed her pretty face. It was her second invitation to dinner. And she was glad she'd refused the first one so she could accept Adam's offer.

CHAPTER FOUR

Promptly at seven that evening Sally took the elevator down to the lobby. Old Jacob Schok eyed her with admiration. "Your dress is good!"

She smiled. It was an ivory silk she'd recently bought. "Thank you," she told the old man. "I hope it's not too fancy."

He shrugged as the elevator came to a halt. "It makes you more beautiful. Who cares about fancy?"

As she stepped from the elevator, she saw Adam just coming in from the street. She had carefully pinned one of his roses to her ivory silk purse. Seeing that he was dressed in a neat dark-blue blazer and gray trousers, Sally was glad that she had dressed up.

Adam smiled when he saw the rose. He said, "You got them in time."

"Very much so," she said. "How nice of you."

"I like flowers," he said casually. "You look great. And I'm taking you to an interesting place."

She laughed. "That won't be difficult. I find everything in Amsterdam interesting."

They walked to an expensive-looking restaurant nearby and he said, "This place specializes in *rijsttafel*."

Her eyes widened. "I'm not sure I know what you mean."

Adam laughed. "You wouldn't be expected to. *Rijsttafel* is a feast the Dutch colonists learned to make in Indonesia. It's popular here in the Netherlands. There's a big assortment of food."

"Something like our buffets at home?" she ventured.

"Yes," he said. "A large dish of rice is surrounded by almost twenty dishes of meats and vegetables and things—and all kinds of tasty sauces."

"I'm not hungry enough for half of that," she protested.

"Just take what you wish," he told her. "I think you'll enjoy it. Try to taste as many things as you can."

And enjoy it she did, treating herself to a taste of this and a bite of that.

Helping himself to a luscious-looking pork concoction, Adam said, "I must apologize for Dorothy again. I gave her a lecture after you left."

"You shouldn't have!"

"I think she acted unpleasantly," Adam said. "And I told her so."

Sally smiled at him. "I'd judge the way she acted with me is typical of how she behaves with other people."

"She can be charming when she likes."

Sally said, "I'm sure of it. But apparently she saw me as some sort of rival."

"Don't be silly. Dorothy and I are just friends. I told you that already."

"Maybe you forgot to tell Dorothy."

"Don't get sassy with me, woman. Or you'll be sorry."

"Does Dorothy know you're dining with me tonight?" Sally persisted.

He hesitated. "I didn't mention it to her. I told her I had to meet someone."

"But didn't say who?"

"No. As a matter of fact, I am expecting someone else to come by. A man who acts as my dealer for paintings in Belgium. I have a list for him of what is available. He promised to come by here and pick it up. He'll only stay a few minutes."

Sally smiled. "At least he will serve as a nice alibi for you."

Adam said, "I don't see it that way. I'll tell

Dorothy tomorrow. I won't try to hide that we met for dinner."

"Perhaps it might be just as well not to mention it," Sally said. "I'll only be here a short time. I don't want to disrupt this long friendship you have with her."

"You won't," he said. "I'm leaving for home soon myself. Soon after I finish the old woman's portrait."

"And when will that be?" she asked.

He sighed. "I should have it done in another two weeks or so. Most of the work has been completed. It will probably take several more weeks for me to pack the other paintings, get my business settled here, and take the plane to New York."

Sally said, "We ought to be returning about the same time."

"Yes. Come to think of it, we will be. I look forward to seeing a lot of you when we get home."

Sally laughed. "Why not? We'll only be a few miles apart."

"A mere nothing," he assured her airily. Then they made idle chitchat about New York. "Now let us try the dessert and coffee," Adam said when they'd finally finished the *rijsttafel*.

It was while they were having coffee that a bearded man came into the restaurant and glanced around. He was wearing a corduroy suit that was rather rumpled. Sally at once thought she remembered him from some-

where else, and then it came to her. He was
the puppeteer near the war memorial.

Adam Bond had also seen him and quickly
got to his feet. "That's my man! I'll give him
the list so he can leave."

"I know him," Sally said. "At least I've seen
him before. He ran the puppet show in the
square. Not far from where you were painting."

Adam looked at her strangely. "You must
be mistaken."

"Are you sure?" she asked.

"Quite sure," he said. "Perhaps this man
may look like the other guy. But it's not the
same person."

She watched Adam go and confer with the
other man for a moment and give him a folded
paper that he took from an inner pocket. She
was convinced the newcomer was the puppeteer and couldn't think why Adam Bond should
deny it. What possible reason could he have?
It was all very strange.

The man left and Adam returned to the table. "He's sending some lists to Belgium tonight. He needed a list of my pictures to add
to the others."

She couldn't get the bearded man out of her
mind. "I'm sorry, but I still think he's the one
who gave the puppet show."

Adam smiled. "The next time you're around
there, I'll have you meet the other guy. They
both have short black beards, but you'll see

they are quite different otherwise."

She shrugged. "Maybe. But at this moment I'd bet anything that they're the same person."

"I hope it's not going to bother you for the rest of the night," he said, ruefully amused. "I'd take you to the square to meet the puppeteer this minute, but he's never there at night. In fact, he isn't always there days, just on certain days."

Sally smiled. "I'll obviously have to take your word for it."

"Then that settles that," he said. "There's a mime show on at a little theater a few blocks from here. Would you care to go?"

"I'm very fond of mime," she said. "And we don't get too much of it in New York."

"Then off we go," he said, rising and helping her from the table.

Darkness had come while they were in the restaurant. They walked hand in hand along the lighted streets. There were a good number of people on the sidewalks and the traffic was heavy, but there was no honking of car horns as one would certainly have heard in New York.

Sally said, "It's quieter here than in Manhattan."

"Yes, just here it is," he told her. "But don't be misled. This is the best part of the city. Amsterdam, like other cities, has its underworld and gangsters to go with it. There are sections I wouldn't dream of taking you."

"I'd rather not think about that," Sally said. "People say just the same things about New York City. But I still love it."

"Large cities are bound to have their bad sides," Adam said.

"But they're so exciting, so full of life and art and ideas, full of hopes and dreams. And I'll bet all cities are different from each other. I know I feel like a different person in Amsterdam."

"It is a different world from America," he said.

Sally asked, "Then you feel it also?"

"Very much so," he said. "The only American I know who lives and thinks exactly as if she were back home is Dorothy Lane. Even her Aunt Vivian is more sensitive to her surroundings."

"I guess Dorothy wants to ignore Amsterdam."

"I get that distinct feeling," Adam agreed. "Just as I feel—though she has many good qualities—she isn't truly interested in my art, it's all pretense. You are able to understand my work. You have good perception."

"Thank you," Sally said. "I told you I think you have great talent and I honestly believe it. It has a very special beauty."

"I don't think Dorothy has ever said that to me," Adam mused. "Though she has talked a lot about the beauty of financial success."

"And she's quite a beauty herself!"

"Granted, she's very beautiful," Adam said as they reached the small theater. "Well, here we are. You'll either love this mime group or you'll be bored silly. Hope it's your cup of tea."

CHAPTER FIVE

Sally and Adam laughed often as they watched the small mime group. Sally thought their humorous interpretations of various types of people—not to mention cats, robots, clocks, and vegetables—were brilliant. The show was over all too soon.

"Thanks for taking me to see that," Sally said as they walked back to her hotel.

"I thought you'd like it," he said. "And I was hoping maybe I could take you someplace tomorrow afternoon."

She shook her head. "I'll be busy. There's a man from Global Airlines interviewing me about my winning the contest. I have to meet him again tomorrow. He's also writing a magazine piece about Americans in Amsterdam."

Adam said, "Isn't that an invasion of your privacy?"

"In a way," she admitted. "But the airline sent him and I guess it's only fair for me to help them with a little publicity material."

"I'd only give him so much time," was Adam's advice. "Is he an American?"

"Yes. His name is Frank Kincaide."

Adam nodded. "I think I've heard of him. He writes a lot of travel pieces for magazines."

"He seems very competent."

Adam eyed her. "I gather he's young and fascinating."

"In his late twenties, I think. He's very nice."

"Be wary," Adam warned. "Those guys are charming until they get you to say something indiscreet. Then they quote you and, believe me, you'll be sorry."

She laughed. "You sound as if you've had a bad experience."

"Several of them," he told her wryly. "I'd expect to find the article praising me as the artist of the decade, and instead I read an account of myself as an eccentric."

They had reached the entrance to Sally's hotel now, and she looked up at him, her attractive face highlighted by the nearby street lamp. "I don't think you're eccentric. I find you different and charming."

He looked pleased. "I'm all for the charming

though I'm not so sure about the different."

"It's meant as a compliment!"

"Then I'll accept it that way," Adam said, looking at her warmly. "This has been a great evening."

"You planned it!"

"And you graced it," he said. "I'm glad you came along, Sally." He drew her close and kissed her with a fiery gentleness.

Sally responded with equal warmth, then finally moved away. "If they can see us inside, they'll think we Americans are even more romantic than the Italians."

"I'll take that risk," Adam said. "When will I be seeing you again?"

"I'm not sure." She hesitated. "I have to meet Frank Kincaide, as I told you. We'll go to lunch and then to a wooden-shoe factory."

Adam gave a mock groan. "That's a tourist thing for sure."

Her eyes twinkled. "Still, it'll make a good publicity picture. I imagine he'll take some photos of me there."

"I think I'd better watch out for that guy," Adam said. "He sounds like a rival for your affections."

She laughed, "Wouldn't that make Dorothy happy?"

"Let's not worry about her," Adam countered with a dismissing wave of his hand. "When do I see you again?"

Sally shrugged. "I'll likely be free tomorrow

evening. But I don't want to interfere with your work."

"You won't," the big blond man said. "Why not come by my studio around six, and we'll go somewhere for a bite. That way I can work right until the last minute."

"Fine," she said. "But you mustn't feel you have to entertain me every night."

"I want to see you," he said. Then he patted her on the arm, kissed her briefly on the cheek, and with a smile went down the street.

The next morning was gray but without any rain. After breakfast Sally took a walk to the square. There was no sign of Adam or of the puppeteer.

After a moment a policeman came strolling by and she hailed him.

"Do you speak English?" she asked.

The officer nodded. "Yes, miss. Can I help you?"

She smiled. "It's only a small thing. I saw a puppeteer here yesterday. He put on a very good show. A man with a short black beard."

"I know who you mean," the officer said with a nod. "But I doubt if you see him here again."

"Oh?"

"He was not one of our regulars," the officer explained. "We get to know the ones who return time after time. I only saw him here two or three times in the last few months. The regulars come more often."

"Thank you for being so helpful," she said. The officer bowed and moved on.

As Sally walked along one of the secondary business streets, she thought about the information he'd given her. Again she was convinced that it was the same man who'd come to meet Adam at the restaurant and get the list from him. Yet Adam had denied this. Had her eyes deceived her or had Adam lied? What reason would Adam have for lying about the man?

At noontime Sally returned to her hotel and freshened up. Then she went down to the lobby. Frank was already there, glancing at his watch.

"I didn't mean to keep you waiting," she said.

The writer smiled. "Not your fault. I arrived here early. I'm going to take you to another favorite place of mine today. It's one of the best eating places in the city."

Sally considered it an adventure just finding the intimate little restaurant. The main entrance was locked, so you had to go around to a side door. Inside was a series of delightful little dining rooms, all connected by steep steps. It was crowded with a prosperous-looking group of patrons conversing fairly loudly.

When they sat down, Frank told her, "Their specialty here is veal with cherries. You might like to try it."

She shook her head. "I'll be able to win a fat-lady contest by the time I get back to New York!"

He laughed. "You could make a new career of it."

"After eating in Amsterdam for a month, I may have to do just that," she said.

Gazing at her across the table, he asked, "Have you made any friends here?"

She nodded. "I've met an artist from New York. He's been here about a year, but he's going back."

The young writer was watching her closely. He said, "His name is Adam Bond."

Sally put down her menu with a small gasp. "How did you know him?"

"I included a mention of him in an article I did about American artists living here."

"I see," she said. "That still doesn't explain how you knew he was my friend."

Frank smiled. "I was driving by your hotel last night. I saw him kissing you."

She sat back. "That was good timing!"

His eyes mocked her. "The press are everywhere!"

CHAPTER SIX

An hour or so later, Sally was being photographed in the wooden-shoe factory. She held up a sample product and stood beside the stout, beaming owner of the place. When they had finished, she and Frank strolled slowly back toward her hotel.

As they walked, she asked, "Does this pretty well wind it up?"

"The interviews?" he said. "Not really. I want a lot more personal stuff for the magazine article. It'll take a while yet."

Her smile was one of astonishment. "Aren't you giving me too much of your time? How can you afford it?"

Frank Kincaide looked smug. "I have a system. I do three or four stories at a time. I'm presently working on three other pieces besides the yarn on Americans in Amsterdam and the PR stuff."

"So that's it," she said. "It sounds like a good plan."

"It works for me," Frank said. "I don't care how long your interviews take. It gives me that much more chance to know you better."

She laughed. "I'm not used to having such interest shown in me."

"You should be," he said. "You're pretty and you're nice. Not too many girls offer that combination."

"Such flattery!"

They halted for a traffic light, and Frank asked, "Did that romantic scene last night mean anything?"

Her eyes widened. "Romantic scene?"

"You know what I mean," he said. "Adam Bond with you in his arms."

"He was just saying good night."

"It looked a lot more than that," Frank said as the light changed and they started across the wide street.

"It wasn't," she assured him. "After all, I only met Adam yesterday."

"You've heard about love at first sight."

"Too risky for me," she said. "I'm the cautious, prudish type."

He glanced at her wryly. "You don't strike me that way."

"I try to hide my hang-ups," she told him.

They reached her hotel and he said, "I won't be able to see you again for a few days. My other assignments are taking me out of the city."

"When will we meet again?" Sally asked.

"I can't say precisely," he said. "But as soon as I get back, I'll be in touch with you."

"Fine," she said with a smile. "I'll miss you. Good luck with your work."

"Watch your step with Adam Bond," he said.

"What do you mean by that?"

"Just a word of warning. You know these impulsive artist types."

His smile was teasing as he gave her a hasty kiss on the lips and then stepped back. "I was only saying goodbye like Adam," he explained and then vanished into the crowd.

Sally found herself amused by his brashness and touched by the fact he was showing so much interest in her. He surely didn't want Adam Bond to get ahead of him as far as she was concerned. She checked at the desk and there were no messages, so she went up to rest for a little before meeting Adam at his studio.

By early evening the sun had come out again, and Sally wore a yellow summery dress under her lightweight jacket. On reaching the studio, she found the blond Adam busily engaged with the finishing touches on Miss Vivian Lane's portrait.

He put palette and brush aside and asked her, "Did you have a good day?"

She told him what she'd done and at the same time examined the large portrait. "It seems done now," she said, staring at it.

Adam stood with her. "No. I want to change the shading on her chin just a little."

Sally smiled at him. "It looks perfect. How does she like it?"

"She's hard to read," the artist said. "She was here to look at it a few days ago. I don't think she hated it, but she didn't offer any raves either."

"It's a fine painting," Sally said, studying it again. "I can't say anything about the likeness, since I haven't met her."

He went across the room to wash his hands in a basin on top of a wooden stand. "You're going to! At least you're going to have the opportunity."

Leaning against the back of a chair as she watched him, she asked, "What do you mean by that?"

He dried his hands and came back to her, smiling. "Dorothy came by earlier. She wants you to have tea with her and her aunt. She's going to leave a message at your hotel desk."

Sally showed surprise. "I can't imagine why she should bother."

"She wants to know you better."

"Oh?"

"Dorothy is a young lady filled with curiosity," Adam went on. "If she thinks she has a rival, she wants to know exactly what she's up against."

"And I'm supposed to be a rival with her, for you?" she said, laughing. "I thought you denied all that."

He said, "Maybe I was wrong." Then he put on his jacket. "You might as well take advantage of the tea, anyway. It will give you a chance to see her aunt. Then you can tell me if I've really captured her on canvas."

"You surely captured Dorothy," Sally said, studying the smaller portrait again.

"I want to do you before you go home," Adam said. "It won't take much of your time."

"I couldn't afford you!" she protested.

"I promise you this will be a bargain," he said. "Tonight we are going to a rather plain place that the newspaper people here go to a lot." And he went to the studio door and held it open.

"Anywhere will do," she told him.

The restaurant proved to be a rather ramshackle place on the waterfront. As they neared it, he looked at Sally with a kind of contained excitement and said, "I have a surprise for you tonight."

She stared at him. "What sort of surprise?"

The blond man said, "I told you my uncle lives and works here in Amsterdam. He's a diamond cutter."

"Yes. You did mention that."

"I've asked him to come here tonight," Adam said. "I want him to meet you. And I'm sure you'll find him interesting."

Sally was at once a little uneasy. "I wasn't expecting this. I won't know what to say or how to act."

He laughed. "Just be yourself. Uncle Theo isn't an ogre. He's a quiet, nice middle-aged man. His full name is Theo Muller and he speaks very good English though he prefers to speak Dutch."

"I'm glad he knows some English," she said. "Because I speak no Dutch at all!"

"It will go fine," Adam assured her, taking her arm as he led her into the restaurant.

The headwaiter knew Adam and at once took him to a booth halfway down the busy room. There, seated at a table, was a tall, thin, gray-haired man. Sally thought his large blue eyes were the saddest she had ever seen. As they approached, he rose and smiled a greeting, and there was a hint of resemblance to his nephew.

"This is the girl I told you about," Adam said. "This is Sally Sheldon."

"My pleasure, Miss Sheldon," the tall, thin man said in a rasping voice. "Adam has been telling me about your being here. How you were fortunate enough to win a contest. Do you enjoy travel?"

"I like it a great deal," Sally said.

They all sat down, and Adam ordered for them.

She found the conversation lagging, so she asked Adam's uncle, "Have you ever been to America, Mr. Muller?"

"No," he said. "And I would like to go. But the time has not yet come."

"I wish he could come over," Adam said. "I hope I can arrange it one day."

"Do not count on it," Theo Muller said. "My friends and my work are here. And Amsterdam is my home."

"I can understand that," Sally said. "But you must come to New York for a visit."

He nodded. "I shall very likely, one day soon." Then he turned to Adam and spoke to him quietly in Dutch. Adam answered him in Dutch, and the conversation went on for several minutes, with Sally being unable to follow any of it.

Adam turned to her apologetically. "That was rude of us. You must forgive me. But we had a rather personal problem to discuss. This way it needn't trouble you."

She smiled. "I don't mind. After all, I'm the intruder."

"That's not so!" Adam protested. "You are here because I wanted you to come and my uncle wished to meet you."

The food arrived at that moment and kept them occupied for a while. Occasionally Adam's uncle would lapse into Dutch again and Adam would answer him in Dutch. But most of the time they spoke in English.

It was while they were having coffee that Adam asked his uncle, "Do you have any of your work to show her?"

Smiling, Theo Muller reached into an inner jacket pocket and brought out a small chamois bag. He carefully placed it on the table in front of Sally and opened it. Revealed were a half-dozen diamonds, sparkling and beautiful.

"They are lovely!" she exclaimed, gazing at them with a kind of fascination.

"I shaped and polished them," the old man said proudly. "You may pick them up and examine them more closely if you wish."

Hesitantly, she picked up one of the stones. Holding it between her thumb and forefinger she admired it.

"I've never seen a stone so lovely!" she exclaimed.

"It is a good one," Theo Muller agreed.

"And Uncle Theo is an expert at bringing out the finest in any stone," Adam said.

Then he spoke to his uncle in Dutch again.

Sally returned the gem and the older man carefully closed the chamois bag and restored it to his pocket.

She said, "I've heard the best diamonds come from here."

"And the best craftmanship is here to shape the stones," Adam told her.

Sally smiled at Theo Muller, saying, "So you are also an artist in your own way, just like Adam." She saw the pleased look this brought to his lined face.

It was just after ten o'clock when they left the restaurant. She noticed the night seemed especially dark, and the streets were no longer busy in this rather shabby neighborhood. Sally strolled along leisurely with Adam on one side of her and his uncle on the other. It was Adam's plan to see his uncle safely back to his boardinghouse and then take her back to her hotel. They followed a street that ran along a canal for a while. Then the older man suggested a side street that would be a shortcut.

This narrow street was dark and deserted, with only an occasional light showing from one of the small brick houses. Suddenly, Sally noticed that Adam was glancing over his shoulder at something.

He gripped her arm and, in a low voice, said, "That small car coming slowly behind us, it's following us, I'm sure!"

"What should we do?" she asked tensely, glancing behind at the menacing black car.

"There's an alley ahead on the right," Adam said. "When we come up by it, we'll turn and run as fast as we can. It's too small for the car, and if they come after us on foot, we won't be any worse off than here."

Adam's uncle spoke tensely. "The diamonds! Someone must have seen them and come after us!"

"Be ready!" Adam warned them. And as they came to the alley, he held Sally's arm and raced ahead into the darkness with her, his uncle coming after them. The middle-aged man tried to keep up with them, but after a moment it was evident he was falling behind.

Gasping, Adam halted and waited for the older man. "Can you keep going?"

"I think so," his uncle said, but his agonized breathing suggested he was wrong.

The three of them crouched low in the shadow of a building. Loud guttural shouts could be heard from the street and then the sound of footsteps on the cobblestones coming after them.

"Come on!" Adam ordered them.

They ran on again, their steps made fleeter by the knowledge the would-be thieves were coming after them. Sally saw Adam's uncle stumble and falter. She halted to take his arm and help him forward.

"Here!" Adam had halted and was pointing to a narrow space, no more than a foot wide, between two of the looming black buildings.

There was no time to question his decision. She ran forward and thrust herself in the small hiding space offered, with Adam's uncle and Adam following her. They stood there in the damp and dark, cramped and fearful. Waiting.

They did not have long to wait. It seemed only a moment later that two men went running by, heading far down the alley. The sound of their running gradually faded, and all was silence again.

Sally whispered, "What now?"

"We must stay where we are for a while," Adam said in a low voice. "Their car will likely be driven around to the other end of the alley and pick them up. When they are sure they have lost us, they will leave."

"I hope it's soon," she said grimly. "I can only think of rats and other awful things being in here!"

The older man next to her gave her a comforting pat on the arm. "Better rats than those thieves. Some of those men can be pretty violent."

"Are both of you all right?" Adam asked.

"I am," Sally said. "Just scared to death."

After a long wait, Adam told them, "I think it's safe to go on." They warily emerged from their hiding place and headed for the street.

There were more dark, silent streets with few house lights but no more unpleasant incidents. Sally's nerves remained taut as they continued. Finally, they reached the large boardinghouse where Theo Muller lived and said good night to him.

The older man told Sally, "I'm sorry this unfortunate business happened."

"Please don't worry about it," she told him.

"You are a fine young woman," he said, bowing. Then he spoke briefly to Adam in Dutch and went toward the house.

They waited until he was safely in before they moved on.

Adam had his arm around Sally as they walked and he said, "You are still trembling a little."

"I hadn't realized," she said.

"I shouldn't have walked you along that route," he said, angry with himself. "I thought the three of us would be safe enough."

"At least you outsmarted them."

"I was afraid for you and my uncle," he said.

"I think you handled it well," she told him.

"We're safe enough now," he said. "We're getting closer to the center of things. How do you like my uncle?"

"I think he's nice," she said. "And he was very brave. He stood up to the danger very well."

"He's been through a lot. During the war—World War II—he was very brave in the Dutch underground fighting the Nazis. And he was only a teenager. And a few years ago both his wife and his son died from a case of food poisoning. He's very lonely now."

"I could sense that," Sally said. "Poor man. Maybe you should encourage him to get married again."

Adam sighed. "I doubt if I'll ever manage that. It would be something if he stopped being so stubborn and started meeting some women."

They were now back in the well-lit area of the city. The streets were no longer deserted. Couples strolled by, occasional cars made an appearance, their headlights adding to the brightness.

Adam told Sally, "My uncle didn't like Dorothy."

"When did he meet her?"

"A little while ago."

She teased him, "So you have him judge all your girl friends?"

"That's not fair," he said.

She laughed. "I don't blame you for wanting his opinion. What didn't he like about Dorothy?"

"He thought her arrogant and unfeeling."

"She does give that impression," Sally admitted. "Yet there are moments when she's not all that bad. According to you."

"I know," he said. "That's why I've kept on being friends with her. But I realize now that may be risky. She's started taking me for granted. Deciding that I'm seriously interested in her. I denied it yesterday. But now I know better."

"And you're not serious?"

"No," he said. "I'm not. By the way, Uncle Theo approves of you."

She raised her eyebrows. "Was that what all that Dutch was about?"

Adam laughed. "A good deal of it."

"That was devious of you," she reprimanded him.

They had reached the entrance of her hotel and were now facing each other.

His expression was serious. "I had to ask him what he thought of you. I'd already told him I was in love with you."

"Adam!" Sally protested. "You haven't even told me that!"

"I'm telling you now."

"Let's not go into that tonight," she said. "Let's give ourselves a little more time."

He was holding her by the arms. "I don't need any more time. I know how I felt when you were in danger tonight. I love you and I want to marry you."

She could not doubt his sincerity. Touched, she murmured, "Adam!"

"And you love me," he said. "I'm certain of it!" He took her in his arms and kissed her again.

At that moment two elderly women entered the hotel. There was subdued laughter from them as they passed the young couple.

Sally gave the big blond man a despairing smile. "You see? You've completely ruined my reputation at the hotel."

"I don't care," he laughed. "If you like, I'll go in and shout that we plan to be married!"

She touched a small hand to his lips. "Not required," she said and eyed him gently.

"Then it's all settled?"

"Don't rush me," she said. "What about Dorothy? Hadn't you better talk to her first?"

He frowned. "Why? I don't need her permission."

"She's not going to be pleased. She may even be badly let down," Sally warned the young artist.

"Look, I never asked her to marry me or even be engaged to me," he said.

"But you did have a friendship, a warm friendship. I think she should first hear about us from you."

Adam sighed. "All right. If that's what you want."

"I'm afraid it has to be," she said.

"I'll do it," he promised. "Give me a day or two." He kissed her again and they said a final good night.

CHAPTER SEVEN

When Sally awoke the next morning, she
saw that the sun was shining again. She
bathed and dressed leisurely, her mind filled
with the events of the night before. It had been
reminiscent of a gangster movie. Never in her
wildest imagination could she have pictured
herself hiding in a tiny space between two
buildings with two men she had known only
a short time, while dangerous pursuers were
on their trail.

But it had happened! Just as exciting had
been Adam's romantic outburst at the end of
the evening. He had been boldly forthright in
asking her to marry him. And she had no rea-

son to doubt that he truly loved her. She was almost equally sure that she was in love with him.

The swiftness with which it had all happened was what made her uneasy. There was lots of talk about love at first sight, and that had almost been the case with them. But Sally worried that they might be allowing their isolation in a foreign land, along with the glamour of their meeting in this setting, to influence their judgment. Would they have fallen in love in the same way if they'd met back in New York City?

She pursued these thoughts in the cafe next door as she had her usual light breakfast. Well, she'd see to it that they didn't rush into marriage too quickly. But she hoped Adam would talk to Dorothy soon.

When Sally had finished breakfast, she returned to the hotel and was surprised to find Dorothy, seated in a chair in the small lobby, waiting for her. Dorothy stood up to greet her with a smile.

"Have you been waiting long?" Sally wanted to know.

Dorothy said, "It gave me a rest and time to go over my shopping list." She was wearing a light-gray suit that must have cost a fortune.

"I haven't really begun to look at the stores yet," Sally confessed.

"Wait until just before you leave, the end of the month. The large stores have sales then.

I do my shopping chiefly at exclusive bou-
tiques," Dorothy informed her.

"How nice for you," she said politely.

"I'm calling on you for my Aunt Vivian,"
the girl said. "She would enjoy having you
come for tea at four."

"You're not far away, are you?"

"Just a few streets back. We're in the Grand
Hotel."

"Well, then that is no problem," Sally said.
"I'd be delighted to meet your aunt."

Dorothy said, "I'm glad you're free. I thought
you might be seeing someone—perhaps Adam
Bond."

"I saw Adam last night," Sally said, wanting to be completely honest about this.

"Did you?" Dorothy looked less happy. "He
told me he was going to meet his uncle."

"He did," Sally said. And she quickly pro-
ceeded to tell the other girl about the exciting
happenings of the night before.

When Sally finished, Dorothy eyed her with
disdain. "I'd say you were all three fools! One
doesn't flaunt gems in those waterfront res-
taurants. There are always weird characters
around."

"I think Adam's uncle will be more careful
in the future," Sally said.

"I should hope so," Dorothy sniffed. "I can
only say I found him rather strange."

Sally smiled. "He seemed a mild, pleasant
man."

"He made me uneasy," the other girl said. "I had the odd feeling he wasn't what he pretended to be."

"He didn't affect me that way," Sally told her.

Dorothy moved toward the street door. "I must be on my way. I've got dozens of things to do. We'll see you at four."

"Yes," Sally said, accompanying Dorothy to the sidewalk. "And do thank your Aunt Vivian. It's really very kind of her."

"She enjoys entertaining any stray Americans who come her way," Dorothy said rather archly, then left.

The Grand Hotel was very old, very exclusive. Sally felt a trifle shabby in her new linen dress, but she tried to fight the feeling. After all, the hotel patrons were extremely wealthy. There was no way her clothes could compare to theirs—even though her outfit was perfectly attractive.

Having inquired about the Lanes' room number, she took the elevator up to the fifth floor and then wandered down the white corridor, with its plush, deep carpeting, until she reached Vivian Lane's suite. She pressed the ivory buzzer and waited.

A maid in a regular black-and-white uniform answered the door, a middle-aged, weary-looking woman. "You must be Miss Sally Sheldon."

Sally managed a smile. "Yes. I see that I'm expected."

The woman nodded. "Do please come in. The ladies are waiting for you."

The suite was as elegant as the rest of the hotel, Sally saw as the maid led her to the sitting room.

Dorothy, a picture in blue, stood up from her chair at a round table. "So glad you were able to come. This is my Aunt Vivian."

"I'm happy to meet you, Miss Lane," Sally said in a hollow voice.

The elderly woman, also seated at the table, studied Sally with piercing eyes. She looked exactly like the portrait Adam had painted of her. In a discreet dark-brown dress, with a high white collar, she was the picture of an aristocrat.

"You're the young woman who won a trip to Holland," Vivian Lane said. "They have contests for everything nowadays."

Her words served as a challenge to bring Sally out of her panic and to a kind of rebellious state of mind. "Since I'm not wealthy like you, Miss Lane, winning a contest was about my only chance of seeing this part of the world."

The old woman's gray eyebrows rose. "Ah! I gather you are one of those young people who don't approve of the wealthy!"

"I neither approve nor disapprove," Sally told her. "I'm sure if I had the money I'd like to spend it on good living just as much as anyone else."

Aunt Vivian considered this and said, "I like that. At least you're honest in your opinions."

Dorothy said, "Miss Sheldon met Adam Bond last night. He introduced her to his uncle and they had a rather awful experience."

The old woman sniffed. "That doesn't surprise me! The world is filled with awful experiences these days!" And she asked Sally, "Tell me what happened."

Sally launched into a quick account of the night's events.

The old woman listened with obvious interest.

Sally ended with, "I think we were very lucky."

"You were all of that," Aunt Vivian said and, indicating a chair to her right, ordered her, "Do sit down here, girl. You tire me standing there!"

Sally smiled at Dorothy and crossed to the designated chair and sat. Dorothy sat down on the other side of her.

In an effort to keep some sort of conversation going, Sally asked something she already knew. "Have you visited Holland many times, Miss Lane?"

The old woman gave her a sharp glance. "I come here every year. I have done so since the end of the Second World War."

Dorothy leaned forward to explain, "My aunt

was engaged to marry a young medical officer. He was killed not far from here in the last days of the war."

"No need to prattle about that!" Aunt Vivian said, giving her niece an angry look. She turned to Sally. "Coming here has become a pleasant way to spend a few months. There's a wonderful doctor here for my arthritis, too. I suppose I shall come here until I'm too old to make the journey."

Sally said, "I don't blame you for liking Holland. It's such a clean, pleasant little country. I'm glad to have had the chance to visit it."

They were interrupted by the weary-looking maid arriving with their tea on a tray. She set the things out and poured their tea, then vanished again.

As she sipped her tea, Sally said, "I've seen the portrait Adam Bond is doing of you, Miss Lane. It is a wonderful likeness."

The old woman frowned. "The young man has a talent, I won't deny that. But I wouldn't have had the portrait done if Dorothy hadn't continually nagged at me. I'm not a pretty woman, and I know it!"

Sally said, "I think your face has character and dignity. It's very striking."

Dorothy was quick to add, "And the family will want something to remember you by."

The old woman sat up straighter and sterner than before and told Dorothy, "My family, what few are left, none closer to me than you,

will be much more interested in the reading
of the bequests I leave for them than in any
artist's likeness of me."

Dorothy's face flushed. "You're so cynical,
Aunt Vivian. You know we all love you."

"I do believe you worry about my longevity,"
the old woman told her. "Let me remind you
I come from long-lived New England stock!"

"You make it sound as if we were talking
about animals not people," Dorothy said, flus-
tered.

"We're talking about the human animal, my
dear niece," the old woman snapped. "And not
always a credit to the planet either!"

"What will Sally think of us!" Dorothy said.

Aunt Vivian shifted her glance to Sally and
said, "I don't think this young lady is any more
sheltered than most of her contemporaries. Tell
me, Sally, do you have a family?"

"My parents have a farm in Iowa. My brother
is a pharmacist in Boston and lives there with
his family."

"Aunt Vivian owns most of the shares of a
big pharmaceutical company in New York,"
Dorothy volunteered.

Her aunt frowned at her. "That is not true.
I happen to own a good share of the company's
stock. A far cry from owning it!"

Dorothy offered Sally an uneasy smile. "Do
you plan to see Adam soon again?"

The question struck her as odd. She said,
"We haven't planned anything. I suppose I will

see him since you and he are among the few people I have met in this city."

"I'd think there would be plenty of young men among the other tourists here," Dorothy suggested, as if hinting that Sally was too interested in Adam to look for anyone else.

Aunt Vivian said, "Why are you questioning the girl this way? What she or Adam Bond does is their business. Unless you've decided to have one of your silly crushes on the young man! In which case I advise you to forget him! No matter how excellent an artist he is, I'm sure he makes very little money."

Dorothy frowned. "Adam is a fine, talented man and I'm certain he does well enough. You disapprove of anyone I happen to meet."

"And I've been right nearly every time," was her aunt's reminder. She pointed a bony finger at Dorothy. "Remember that bogus count last year?"

"He didn't really fool me," Dorothy insisted. "I guessed all along he was a fake."

"Not before you nearly drove me mad with your dreams of going home a baroness or a countess or whatnot," her aunt said sternly. "You never show any judgment."

Sally found herself an unwilling partner to this exchange, which she felt was both pathetic and amusing, in view of the fact Adam had declared his love for her.

She glanced at her wristwatch and said, "I'm sorry. But I really must go."

Aunt Vivian nodded. "Very well. I have enjoyed your visit. You must come again."

"Thank you," Sally said, rising. "I've also been pleased to meet you."

"Dorothy will show you out," the old woman said, her voice betraying signs of tiring. "At this time in the afternoon, I find myself weary."

Sally let Dorothy take her out to the hallway and said, "It was good of you both to entertain me," she said.

Dorothy was much more her arrogant self away from her aunt's presence. She said, "It gave me a chance to know you better."

Sally smiled. "We should see each other again. There are so many places I want to go. I'm sure you're familiar with many of them."

"We'll see," Dorothy said carefully. "I want to be your friend. But I don't think it's possible unless you keep in mind that Adam Bond is important to me. I've known him for some time."

"I realize that," Sally said with an innocence that wasn't altogether sincere. She knew what the other girl was hinting even though she decided it was best at this point to pretend not to.

Dorothy's tone became hard as she went on, "You heard what I said to Aunt Vivian. I'm interested in Adam."

Sally went on playing her innocent role. "I'm sure he's just as interested in you."

"Don't be such a little fool!" the auburn-girl

snapped at her. "I'm telling you that I may want to marry Adam."

Sally stared at her. "You're in love with him?"

"I didn't say that," Dorothy sputtered. "I said I may decide to marry him. I know he's deeply in love with me. And I think I can help him in his career."

"But isn't that just between you and Adam?"

Dorothy bit her lip. "I suppose so. I only wanted to make it clear to you."

"You have," Sally assured her, hoping the auburn-haired girl would end the conversation.

"Very well," Dorothy said. "I'll judge your attitude by the way you act. I'd rather you didn't go out with Adam again unless I'm with him. If you keep that condition, I'm sure we can be good friends."

"You're very kind," Sally said, amused by the irony of it all.

"I'll be in touch with you in a few days," Dorothy promised. "We can talk some more then."

Sally made her way to the elevator, feeling they had talked quite enough. She dearly wished the subject of Adam hadn't come up, but it was Dorothy who had been responsible for it. Sally feared it would only make things worse when Dorothy was told by the young artist that he planned to marry someone else. And she was that someone else!

It was late afternoon when Sally reached the hotel.

Old Jacob Schok was on elevator duty and took her up to her floor. He said, "You had a visitor this afternoon."

"I did?" she said, surprised. "Was it the writer, the man with the camera?"

The old man shook his head. "I have never seen him before. I told him you were not in, but he insisted on going up to your room. He was large with a red face and a small mustache."

"What did he do when he found I wasn't in?"

"I'm not sure," the old man said. "I was called on to serve a guest some food from the cafe next door. When I do room service, the boy operates this elevator."

"So you don't know when this man left?"

"No," Jacob said. "I did not see him leave."

"Did the boy say anything about him?"

"I asked him," the old man said, "but he didn't remember anyone to fit the description."

"Strange!" she said.

"Yes, miss. That is why I mentioned it," the elevator operator said.

He let her out and she went to her room. As she placed her key in the lock, the door swung open. It had been open when she reached it. She slowly stepped inside and gazed about the small room.

She gasped as she saw that every drawer of

the dresser had been opened and ransacked.
Fifty dollars had been taken. Her closet was
open and her clothes were carelessly strewn
about, as if the intruder had gone about a
relentless search for something.

Tears of anger and frustration coursed down
her cheeks. Then she rushed back to the elevator and rang for it. When it arrived, she got
on and told the troubled Jacob, "I've been
robbed! That man somehow got into my room
and went through all my things!"

CHAPTER EIGHT

Sally's news put the lobby in an uproar. She told the details to the hotel manager and he came up and saw the damage done for himself. Then it was downstairs again to have the telephone operator put a call through to the police. Sally also tried to reach Adam at his studio, but no one answered the phone.

The police sent a plainclothes officer to investigate, and he went up to her room with her and took notes on everything. He was a short, sober-faced man who seemed in a perpetually gloomy mood.

"This was easy," he assured her in his perfect English. "They get hotel keys and make copies of them. From time to time, they later make raids on the rooms in various hotels. Obviously some crook has a key to this room."

"I won't feel safe here again," Sally said tautly.

The little man looked bored. "No need to panic. The hotel is going to install a padlock on the outside which you can lock when you're not here. When you are inside, all you need do is slip the bolt in place and no one can enter regardless of how many keys they might have."

"I've never experienced anything like this before," she told the officer.

"Have you lost anything of value?"

"About fifty dollars. I had all my other money with me in travelers' checks," she said.

"Then you were lucky. No clothing or jewelery gone?"

"I have little jewelery. Just some fake things, which they didn't bother with. All my clothes were gone over, but they're safe."

The little man continued to look grim. "Apparently, whoever it was tried to find something which wasn't here. Probably more money."

"You think so?"

He nodded. "These thieves are chiefly out for money and precious stones such as diamonds."

This struck a note in her mind. She remembered the incident of the previous night and quickly told the plainclothes man what had happened.

He listened impatiently. Then he said, "I can say your friends were foolish in allowing the diamonds to be seen in a public place. But I much doubt there is any connection with your room being ransacked and what happened last night."

She tried to comfort herself by saying, "The thieves couldn't know I was staying here."

"Exactly," he said. "I will report what has happened and do what I can about it. Do not expect too much."

Sally saw him to the door. "Just as long as it doesn't happen another time."

"If you take precautions, I'm certain it won't," the plainclothes man said. "I trust your other experiences in Amsterdam will be more pleasant."

Sally thanked him and, after she saw him out, carefully closed her door. Everything had happened so swiftly, it had given her little time to try and think it out. Her head was aching and she was beginning to feel hungry. She went downstairs and out to the nearby cafe and had some food and a cup of strong coffee. By the time she returned to the hotel, the porter had installed the new padlock on her door and he gave her the key. She tried to reach Adam on the phone at the desk before going upstairs, but again there was no answer.

In a mood of deep depression, she had Jacob Schok take her up in the elevator.

Sally had a miserable, restless night, waking up several times in a fright. Only toward dawn did she get a real bit of relaxed sleep.

As soon as she had breakfast, she tried to reach Adam on the phone again. This time she got him.

"I tried to get you all last night," she told him.

"Sorry," he said. "I was invited out by an artist friend and I stayed at his place until all hours."

"Something terrible happened here," Sally said. "Someone came to my room and ransacked it and robbed me."

"I can't believe it," he said in dismay.

"It's true," she said unhappily. "That's when I tried to reach you."

"Are you at the hotel now?"

"Yes. At the desk."

"Stay there in your room," he instructed her. "I'll come over at once."

Somehow just talking with him made her feel better. She went back up to her room and waited. She felt that Adam would understand and make everything right. She no longer had the dread feeling of facing an unknown danger alone.

She sat there for a fairly long time going over the details of what had happened. She was able to make nothing of it; it remained just as mysterious as before.

Then she heard an agitated knock on her door and walked toward it. "Is that you, Adam?"

"Yes," he replied in his familiar voice.

With a gasp of relief, she unbolted the door and threw her arms around him. "You don't know how glad I am to see you!"

"And I to see you," the young artist said.

She led him into the room and related everything. She ended with, "All I lost was fifty dollars, which I may have told you already. The worst thing is the fear this has brought."

Adam paced up and down. "I can understand," he said. "But you should be safe enough now."

Sitting on the edge of the bed, she gave him a questioning look as she asked, "Do you think it might have any connection with those men who came after us?"

"I think not," he said.

"The police officer felt the same way," she said. "So it had to be one of those random things, it happening so soon after the other incident being just a coincidence."

The blond man smiled at her. "I'd say that was about it. Your best bet is to put the whole thing out of your mind."

Her smile was bleak. "I hope I may be able to."

"You will," he promised. "And I will do my best to help. By the way, I hear you had tea with the Lanes yesterday afternoon."

"Who told you?"

"Dorothy. Who else? She called after you left and before I went out to keep my appointment with my friend. She didn't seem in the best of humor and she wanted to see me last night. I told her there was no chance."

Sally smiled wryly. "I gather that went down well."

"She tried hard to get me to change my plans, but I simply said I couldn't."

"I imagine she'll blame me. Have all kinds of fantasies about your being out with me!"

Adam said, "You truly think that?"

"Yes."

"I asked her what sort of impression you made on the old lady and she didn't give me any kind of satisfactory answer. Just brushed the question aside."

Sally shrugged. "Perhaps her Aunt Vivian liked me too well to suit her. I found the old woman shrewd and amusing."

"I feel the same way about her," he agreed. "I'll be glad when I have the portrait finished and deliver it. I always have the fear she'll change her mind and not want it. And I badly need the money her painting will bring me."

"She'll keep to her bargain," Sally predicted. "She's that sort of person."

He was standing by the window looking out at the rather dreary courtyard. "What did Dorothy have to say to you?"

"It's just as I suspected," she warned him. "She's sure you're in love with her and she can have you if it happens to be her whim."

The young artist faced Sally, looking angry. "I must say that is flattering."

"There's no other way of putting it. It is almost exactly what she said."

Adam said, "But I've given her no reason."

She got up and faced him. "Think about it. You two have been together a lot."

"Suppose we have?"

"She did get you her aunt's painting to do, and you did Dorothy's portrait as a labor of love. She thinks you adore her."

He groaned and began to pace again. "This is the worst yet!"

"There's more," Sally warned him.

"More?"

"Yes. She warned me not to interfere. Practically accused me of trying to break you two up."

"But I'm in love with you! I've told you that!" he protested.

"I know," she said. "That didn't make it any easier. I had a hard time getting away from her without telling her."

"I wish you had!"

Sally shook her head. "I still say that is your

job. You must straighten it out with her first."

He placed a hand across his eyes and groaned. "I know! And I intend to tell her!"

"When?" she asked quietly.

"In a few days," he said, giving her a pleading look. "Give me a chance. Let me handle this my way."

"I think it would be better for all of us if you saw her and straightened it out right away," Sally told him.

"I know what you think," he sighed and patted her on the arm. "Have a little faith in me and give me credit for some judgment."

Sally said, "I think the longer the confusion goes on, the worse it will be. Perhaps we shouldn't see each other until you clear the decks with Dorothy."

"But I'm innocent in all this," he said unhappily. "I'm the victim of her neurotic ideas. She's thoroughly spoiled and thinks she can manipulate people as she used to do with her dolls. She's a grown-up lady now and it makes a difference."

Sally smiled. "You might try telling her that."

"First, let's find a little relief from all this pressure," the young artist said. "Let's get away from here for the day! Leave Amsterdam and all our woes behind us!"

"It sounds wonderful, but how?"

"We'll rent a car and drive to a little village

about twenty miles from here," he said. "It has windmills and all the trappings of the Old Holland. The people there dress in the native costume and it's like another world. There's a marvelous flower area and even a small zoo. You'll love it!"

And love it she did. The men and women in their quaint, old-fashioned dress and wooden shoes set the tone for the village with its windmills, tulip squares, and canals. There were a number of eating places along with interesting little shops with tourist offerings and some with genuine antiques. The village was crowded with people from all over the world.

At lunchtime Sally and Adam chose to eat in a replica of an old-fashioned tavern. The food was tasty but a little heavy.

"Use lots of cream on your dessert," Adam urged her with a smile. "It's an old Dutch custom."

"I think you've made that up because you like cream," she accused him even as she obeyed him.

He said, "Too bad we can't live in a storybook world all the time."

Sally gave him a reproving smile. "Wouldn't that be running away from reality?"

He looked at her. "Would that be such a crime? Considering the reality we know today."

"I think so," she said. "We should never sub-

stitute a world of make-believe for the real
one. At least not for long. It's taking the easy
way out."

He winced and asked. "Are you saying that
is what I'm trying to do?"

She smiled again. "We all have a tendency
to try it."

"Thanks," he told her. "Good to know I'm
not alone."

"Far from it," she said. "I'm delighted to be
here, with all the ugly and unfinished things
behind me. But I know I must go back."

He nodded. "I arranged to return the car by
five."

"We still have a couple of hours here before
we begin the drive home," Sally said.

"Why didn't I meet you before I met Dorothy, and we'd have saved so much trouble?"
he wondered dismally.

"That's the way life is," she said, wryly
amused. "I think Dorothy will be much less
of a problem for you when you face her with
the truth."

"You're right," he said, his mood changing
and his smile returning. "Now let's go back
and play at darts before the afternoon is over
for us. I used to be a wizard at it."

He actually was pretty good. But she turned
out to be the winner. There was a lot of laughing and joking about that. Eventually, it was
time for them to go to their car and drive back
the busy road to Amsterdam.

They had dinner together in a restaurant close to her hotel and she could sense the young artist's mood becoming more tense now that they were back in the city.

Abruptly Adam gazed at Sally across the table and demanded, "If something happened concerning me that you didn't understand, would you condemn me? I mean, if I weren't able to explain what seemed a wrong."

His question caught her off-guard. She wrinkled her brow as she said, "I'm not certain I follow you."

He kept his eyes fixed on hers. "I'm saying, suppose I might seem to be involved in something bad. And suppose I gave you no practical explanation. Would you give me the benefit of the doubt?"

Sally hesitated. "It's hard to say. It would depend on what you were supposed to have done."

"If you didn't know the facts."

"Then it would be difficult," she said.

"People in love are supposed to fully trust one another," the young artist told her earnestly. "Isn't it a matter of whether you loved me or you didn't?"

She smiled ruefully. "You're trying to stack all the cards against me."

"No. I'm trying to find out what you might do," Adam said.

"Since I believe I love you," she said, "any decision involving you becomes complicated by that love. Making a decision against you would be terribly difficult."

"So you wouldn't jump to any rash conclusions."

"I would hope not."

He reached across and took her hand in his. "You don't know how much better you've made me feel. I know now I have your full trust."

"You've always had that," she said quietly. "But I must admit I still don't know what you're talking about."

"Fancies, my dear," he said lightly. "Mere fantasies. Nothing you should allow to upset you."

"I thought we were back in the real world," she said with a smile.

"And so we are."

"And tomorrow you'll try and see Dorothy and talk with her," she said.

"Seeing her will be easy. Talking to her will be another matter," the artist said dismally. "But I know you are right."

"I'll wait to hear from you," Sally said.

"I'll either come by the hotel sometime during the day or phone a message to the desk for you," he promised.

She nodded. "We'll be a lot happier and able to make plans when it's all settled."

He saw her back to the hotel and held her in his arms and kissed her good night. "Just be patient," he told her. "Soon everything will be fine with us."

"I know," she said, filled with the happy knowledge that he truly loved her.

This euphoria she felt lasted long after she reached her room. Adam had shown a different side of himself during the day, a view which she much enjoyed. The dedicated young artist could place all his ambition aside and enjoy the lighter things of life to the full. It was the mark of a true man of talent.

He had promised to see Dorothy tomorrow and straighten things out with her. Then he and Sally could more openly proclaim their love. All seemed well, except for one tiny shadow. The odd way he had suddenly changed his mood and brought up the question of her trusting him in the face of some strong evidence of evil against him. She couldn't think what he had meant.

Long after she had turned out the lights and placed her head on the pillow, she worried about this puzzle. She finally decided it must have been his way of telling her that he felt trust was an important part of loving. Something with which she could surely agree. And with this happy decision reached, she slipped into a peaceful sleep.

The next morning Sally made the rounds of several of the more centrally located art galleries that she had missed, buying souvenir cards of the works she admired the most.

When she returned to the hotel, old Jacob Schok was on elevator duty. She asked him,

"Did any visitors come for me?"

The old man shook his head. "None, miss. No callers and no phone messages at the desk, as far as I know."

She managed a smile for him. "It seems I've been deserted."

"Not a pretty lady like you," the old man said gallantly as he took her up to her room.

She sorted out her treasures of the morning and then went out for a light midday meal. Sally had decided that Adam wasn't going to get in touch with her until later in the day. It was so like him to put off facing Dorothy until the last moment.

So she kept herself busy for the afternoon. But when evening arrived and there was still no word from Adam, she began to worry. She tried to phone him at his studio and there was no answer.

Growing gradually more uneasy, she remained in her room all evening watching television. She went down to the desk at intervals and tried Adam's number. And always it was the same; the phone rang repeatedly and no one answered. She made her last call at midnight, to the mild astonishment of the night clerk. This call, like the others before it, proved futile. Adam wasn't at home or he wasn't answering his phone. Either way, she couldn't understand it.

CHAPTER NINE

It was an afternoon several days later. Sally and Frank Kincaide were seated on a bench in the public square. It was another of those rather somber days with a threat of rain in the offing and cool enough for her to wear a light raincoat.

The young writer gave her a reproachful glance as he said, "I go away for a few days on assignment, and when I come back, I find you in all this trouble."

She sighed. "I shouldn't have told you."

"You most certainly should have," he said with unusual severity. "I am one of your contacts with the airline. I still have to finish my

PR material on you. In a way, I feel sort of responsible for you."

Sally gave him a grateful look. "That is kind of you. But you really don't have any responsibility for me at all. You mustn't worry yourself about my affairs."

The young man shook his head. "You know that I can't help worrying about you. All this talk about diamonds and would-be thieves following you. Your hotel room ransacked and now Adam Bond vanishing for several days without leaving any word for you."

"I can't understand that," she said.

"What I can't understand is why his disappearance has to mean so much to you?" Frank said. "Why are you so worried about him?"

"He is my friend."

"So am I. Would you worry that much about me under the same conditions?"

She protested weakly, "But these aren't the same conditions. Adam left without warning. And I expected to see him the next day."

"There could be reasons," he said.

"I don't know of any," she told him.

Frank sat back against the bench with a sigh. "It's June, almost the middle of your vacation. You're supposed to be enjoying the experience of a lifetime. And what are you doing? Worrying about a man you've not known more than a few days."

"I've known him for more than a week!" she said in argument.

"All right," the young writer said wearily. "I still question that you should spoil your vacation with concern for his welfare. I'm sure he'll turn up hale and hearty."

"I hope so," she said.

"You look pale and almost ill," he worried. "You must stop all this nonsense. He's probably gone off with some girl. Maybe that wealthy American, Dorothy Lane, who knew him long before you came here."

"No!"

His eyebrows raised. "You seem very certain. Have you tried to contact her?"

"I haven't," she said. "But I'm certain they're not together."

"Why?"

"Because he's not in love with her. He's in love with me," she blurted out.

Frank showed surprise. "That's news! What makes you so sure?"

She looked away, concentrating on some pigeons looking for crumbs. In a small voice, she said, "Because he told me he loved me and asked me to marry him."

"He actually proposed to you?"

"The night before he vanished," she said.

"But you've known him such a little time." Frank couldn't seem to understand it.

"Long enough," she said miserably.

"Seemingly for you," the young writer said. "I've known some people all my life and still don't feel I have much real perception of their characters."

"It's different when you're in love!"

"It must be," he said, his tone of derision showing his outraged state of mind. "I wonder if the airline ever thought of this kind of complication when they started this contest."

"I don't care about the airline. They don't own me!"

"True," he said.

"I'm sorry I ever won the old contest!" she said. "That I ever came to Amsterdam!"

"Stop!" the young writer said. "Go on this way and you'll ruin my travel article."

"I don't care about your precious story!"

"I do and so does the magazine staff. They want me to report you as having a glamorous time here. Not sitting sniveling at the end of a bench!"

She turned on him angrily. "I don't snivel!"

"Well, you're indulging in some sort of strictly girlish grief," the young writer said unhappily. "If I don't watch out, you'll make me the villain in all this."

She said, "You haven't been all that kind to me."

"I'm trying to understand; it isn't easy," he told her.

"It's simple enough. Adam proposed to me

and then vanished the next morning."

There was a long moment of silence from Frank. Then he moved close to her and placed an arm around her shoulders. "I'm sorry. That really must be rough on you. I shouldn't have been so boorish. You say no phone calls to his studio have been answered, and when you went there, the place was locked up?"

"Yes."

Frank thought for a moment. "I don't know why I'm bothering to try to help find him. In a way, he's a good riddance. I could care for you a lot more than he does."

"How can you say that?"

"I wouldn't run out on you without a word."

"He may not have, either. He may have been held up and killed, or somesuch awful thing. I dream about dreadful things happening to him every night."

"A hangover from your fleeing from those thieves," the young writer said. "Let's go at this in a rational way. First, let's list the people who know Adam well and who might be aware of what has happened to him. Now give me some names."

Sally did.

"Well, we can't start with Dorothy Lane," Frank said.

"I don't want to approach her," Sally said tautly. "But there is his uncle. The one who works for the diamond merchants."

"Very good," Frank said. "I'd forgotten him. Perhaps it might be best to get in touch with him first."

"I'd rather question him than Dorothy."

"We'll still have to see Dorothy if the uncle isn't able to give us any information," Frank warned her. "Do you know where the man works?"

"No," she said. "But I can take you to his boardinghouse."

"Then that should be our first move," Frank said. "We can go to his place when we're reasonably sure he's home from work. Sometime in the evening."

"I'm glad you've decided to help me," she told him. "I'd never be able to carry out any plan on my own."

Frank rose. "Of course, you would. You're underestimating your abilities."

Also on her feet now, she smiled ruefully. "At the moment I feel I have no ability or even any courage."

He took her by the arm and guided her toward the street. "I think you have plenty of courage but perhaps lack a little something in judgment."

"You would," she said, managing a small smile again. Just knowing they were going to do something about Adam's being missing made her feel better.

Frank saw her to the hotel and told her, "I'll

be back around seven to pick you up for our visit to Theo Muller."

"Can you spare the time?" she worried. "You must have many more important things to do."

"None, not a one as important as protecting you and your future happiness," he said with more sentiment than he usually revealed. He kissed her cheek lightly.

"You won't be late," she said. "I'll try to reach Adam on the phone before you return."

"Do," he agreed. "That's a good idea. He might suddenly come back."

But Sally had no luck. Three times she tried to get Adam on the phone. Still there was no answer.

CHAPTER TEN

That evening, Sally waited in the lobby for Frank's return, puzzled and more than a little frightened. She remembered the strange questions Adam had asked her about trusting him. They had at least seemed odd then, but she wondered if he'd known something like this might come up, if he'd been trying to prepare her for it.

She had not heard from Dorothy Lane, but there was no reason why the attractive girl should try to reach her. Dorothy might be trying to get in touch with Adam on her own and not succeeding. She might even be blaming Sally for his absence.

While Sally was standing there, filled with doubts, Frank Kincaide come into the lobby. He crossed to her with a wry smile on his face.

"I wish you'd worry about me the way you're worrying about him," he said.

She managed a half smile for him. "You haven't asked me to marry you."

"I would," he told her. Glancing over at old Jacob Schok, who was watching them with interest, he said, "Let's make plans. The elevator man can be the best man!"

"You!" she said. "Stop teasing. I tried to get Adam on the phone again. It was just the same. No one there."

"I expected that," he said. "So now it's our job to find his uncle."

"Yes."

"You're sure you know the house?" Frank asked.

"Positive," she said. "We stood there for a little while the night we walked him home. I noticed the surroundings."

"Fine," Frank said. "Then let's go."

They drove to the street in his rented car. Then he parked it and they walked past several houses.

"This is the one, I'm sure of it," she said, pointing out a four-storied brick house.

"Looks as if there could be a lot of people living there," he said bleakly. "Let's see what we can find out. There must be some sort of landlady."

The hallway was spartan but clean. Frank knocked on several doors, making inquiries. The landlady was away. But they were directed to a door at the rear of the stairway. It was said to be the apartment of the caretaker.

Frank knocked on the door and told Sally, "This could be where our luck takes a turn."

"I hope so," she said.

The door opened and a rather gaunt young woman with a child in her arms stood gazing at them. She asked in Dutch, "Do you want some help?"

"Yes," Frank replied in English. "We're looking for a middle-aged man. A tenant in this house."

"Ah!" the young woman replied in English. "I will call my husband. He knows all the tenants." And she walked back inside.

A moment later a stout young man appeared, looking annoyed and sleepy, as if his wife had just awakened him, which was probably the case.

He frowned at them and asked, "What do you want?"

Frank said, "We're looking for a man. He lives here."

The man yawned and asked, "What is his name?"

Sally spoke up. "His name is Theo Muller. He is a diamond cutter."

The stout caretaker scowled. "We have no such man here."

"You must have!" Sally insisted. "I saw him walk into this house."

"I cannot help what you saw," the caretaker said. "There is no Theo Muller living at this address!" And he slammed the door in their faces.

Frank looked at her grimly. "Pleasant chap!"

"He has to be wrong!" she protested. "I saw Theo Muller come into this very building."

The young writer gave her a skeptical look. "The caretaker ought to know who lives here."

"I still think he isn't telling us the truth," she insisted.

Frank took her arm and led her out to the street. As they walked back to the car, he said, "We're probably going too far with this, anyway. We don't know that any harm has come to Adam Bond. He may be away from his studio for perfectly normal reasons."

"He would have let me know," Sally worried.

"Don't be so sure," Frank warned her. "I think the best thing we can do now is get back in the car and return to your hotel." He opened the car door for her.

"I'm sorry I've wasted your time," she said as she stepped inside.

He smiled down at her. "Any time spent in your company is not wasted." With that, he closed the door and got in beside her.

She stared at the house on the hillside above

them and said, "I counted so much on talking to Adam's uncle."

"Who doesn't seem to exist, at least not at that address," her companion said.

"There has to be an answer."

"If you think of it, let me know," Frank said wryly. And he turned on the ignition key of the little car.

At precisely that moment Sally saw a figure she recognized come walking slowly along the sidewalk toward where they were parked.

She hastily placed a hand on Frank's arm and told him excitedly, "Don't drive away! I see him! Adam's uncle! He's walking toward us now!"

"Are you sure?" Frank wasn't convinced, but he did shut off the engine.

"Yes," she cried and quickly let herself out of the car and ran along the sidewalk in the near darkness to greet the man.

When she came face to face with him, she could see that he looked astonished and actually frightened.

"Miss Sheldon," he said tensely.

"Yes. Sally," she said. "I've been trying to find you, Mr. Muller. I went to your boarding-house. They told me there was no one there by your name."

The man listened nervously. "Did they say that?"

"Yes," she said. "Why did they lie?"

"I asked them to," Theo Muller said in an uneasy tone.

At that moment Frank came up and joined them.

The older man stared at him. "Who is this?"

"A friend," she said. "He volunteered to come with me." She turned to Frank and said, "Mr. Muller asked them not to reveal that he lives up there."

Frank scowled. "They followed your instructions. Have you some reason for not wanting it known where you live?"

"I will be honest with you," the man said. "I was once a gambler. Mixed up with a bad crowd. I am no more. But they continued to keep after me, to bother me. To elude them, I changed my address and came to live there on the hill. Why did you come to see me?"

"Because of Adam," she said. "He's vanished. Been gone for several days. And he promised to see me the morning he disappeared."

The older man seemed to become less tense. He said, "You mustn't be concerned about that. Quite often Adam is called to visit Berlin and even Paris in a hurry to evaluate some art collection. He is one of the few experts on eighteenth and nineteenth century Dutch painters."

"But he left no word for me! Not even a note!" she sighed.

"When a large auction is scheduled, there

is sometimes little time to spare. Adam was likely summoned to one of the larger cities to do some appraisals. I've known him to be away a week on such errands," the old man explained.

Sally said, "I knew nothing about that."

"And he most likely forgot that he hadn't told you," Theo Muller said. "There is no reason at all to be concerned about him. I promise he'll return with a full explanation very shortly."

The older man sounded so sincere it was difficult to doubt him.

With a sigh, she said, "Very well. I'll wait and see. At least you know he is away."

"I wish I could do more to help," Theo Muller apologized. "If you need to see me again, it would be best to come to the Berkhim Brothers, Diamond Merchants. That is where I spend my working hours." He gave her the address.

Frank gave Sally a grim smile. "Satisfied?"

"I suppose so," she said.

She thanked Adam's uncle and they walked with him as far as their car. Then he said good night and left them to make his way up the hill to the boardinghouse.

Frank stood watching his slowly retreating figure and said, "You were right about one thing. He does live there."

"Let's go," she said wearily, sick of the whole business.

When they reached the area where her hotel

was located, Frank took her to a coffee shop.

Over his steaming cup, he said, "Well, I hope you're finally satisfied."

Sally shrugged. "What his uncle said may be true."

"Why doubt it?"

"It's just not like Adam to leave so abruptly," she said. "And then that business of his uncle having his name concealed bothers me."

Frank said, "It shouldn't. People can get mixed up with a bad crowd. And then you have to work very hard to get out of their clutches. It does happen, you know."

She smiled wryly. "I don't have your expert knowledge of how things work here, I guess."

"I'm afraid not," he said. "What a story I'm going to write about you! Contest winner finds romance in Amsterdam!"

"Don't you dare write that!" she protested.

He laughed. "Well, isn't it true?"

"Only partly," she said. "Actually, I may never see Adam Bond again. He likely has had second thoughts about asking me to marry him and he's run away."

"The hero runs away," he said. "That wouldn't make any kind of a story."

"It begins to look a lot nearer the truth," she said.

Frank's eyes met her in a teasing fashion as he inquired, "Why not let me take over the role of the hero?"

She gave him an amused look. "You're not really serious about that?"

"Of course I am," the young writer said. "I thought of you continually when I was away."

"You're really ready to take over from Adam?" she asked. "Ready to ask me to be your wife?"

The smile on his face became wary, and then he said, "Why not? Marry me, Sally!"

"You're mad!" she said, laughing.

He proved his recklessness by leaning forward, placing an arm around her, and kissing her before the eyes of the interested waiter and all the others at the crowded counter.

CHAPTER ELEVEN

The next morning Sally again tried to reach Adam Bond by phone without success. Frank Kincaide was busy for the day on another assignment, and she felt desolate and very much alone. On impulse she decided to phone Dorothy. There was a small chance the auburn-haired girl might have some news about Adam.

When it came to actually making the call, Sally almost changed her mind, knowing how cold and arrogant Dorothy could be when she wished. But Sally forced herself and a moment later a weary voice answered at the other end.

Sally asked, "May I speak with Miss Dorothy Lane?"

There was a silence and then the voice said with a Dutch accent, "That is not possible."

"I'm sure she'll be glad to hear from me. We're friends," she persisted.

The female voice informed her, "You will please wait one minute."

Sally waited, feeling sure that she had won over the maid. Within a few minutes, she would be speaking with Dorothy. But when a new voice came at the other end of the line, Sally recognized it as belonging to Dorothy's Aunt Vivian.

The old woman asked, "Who is calling?"

"Sally Sheldon," she said. "I had tea with you the other day."

"Tea!" the old woman said as if searching her mind. Then, suddenly, she went on, "Of course! The contest girl!"

"Yes," she said, knowing that was how the stern old woman would always think of her.

"Dorothy is not here," the voice went on. "She is in Paris on one of her shopping sprees!"

Sally was stunned to hear this, in view of the fact that Adam Bond was also out of town. She said, "I didn't know she was planning any such trip."

"My niece never plans anything!" Aunt Vivian said in an acid tone. "She suddenly decides she wants to do some shopping and off she goes."

"When do you expect her back?"

"When she appears. She's supposed to be

back tonight, but I'm not counting on it," the old woman said.

"Did she go alone?" Sally asked cautiously, knowing this was a most important question.

"No," Dorothy's aunt said. "She took the young woman who helps her buy her clothes with her. To act as a guide and adviser."

This news brightened Sally a good deal. It suggested that the auburn-haired girl had not gone off with Adam, as she'd begun to think for a few moments.

Sally said, "Well, I'll call her later."

"What are you doing for lunch?" Aunt Vivian demanded.

"I have no real plans."

"Then have it with me," the old woman said sternly. "Be here at one sharp."

"Are you sure I won't be a nuisance?" Sally worried.

"If I felt you'd be a nuisance, I wouldn't ask you," Dorothy's aunt snapped. Then she hung up the phone.

"Madame is awaiting you in the sitting room," the maid said when Sally appeared at the hotel suite with a bouquet of wildflowers.

Aunt Vivian was seated in a high-backed chair, the thick gray hair perfectly styled, her patrician face showing a slight smile.

"My dear! How sweet of you to join me," the old woman said.

Sally said, "It is I who must thank you. And

I hope you'll enjoy these wildflowers." She handed the small bouquet to the woman.

Aunt Vivian smelled the tiny wildflowers and showed delight. "I love wildflowers," she declared. Holding out the bouquet for the maid, she ordered, "Do please place them in a vase and then bring them back for the table."

As the maid vanished with the flowers, Sally said, "It's a nice walk here from my hotel."

"Do sit down opposite me," Dorothy's aunt said. "The luncheon will be served on the table here."

Sally obediently sat in the chair across the table from the stern older woman.

Aunt Vivian was studying her. "You know you're a most attractive young woman," she said. "I expect that's why the airline chose to give you their prize."

Embarrassed, she said, "No. In fact, they never saw me until after I won the contest."

"Well, you could have won it on good looks," her hostess said. "Of course, my Dorothy is a beauty, but what is the value of it? She doesn't know how to make the best of herself."

Sally said, "She is beautiful."

"Bad disposition," Aunt Vivian said. "Mind you, she's not to be given all the blame. I spoiled her. Her parents died when she was young. She's missed them. And worst of all they left her a lot of money that she now has fully in her control."

Sally smiled. "So she is able to indulge in shopping sprees."

"Yes. She wouldn't be if I held the purse strings, but I don't. Of course, virtually all my money will go to her one day. But she has so much of her own, she won't even notice it."

"That's too bad," Sally observed, thinking this was a world to which she'd had little access before.

The fierce old eyes studied her. "What are your prospects, my girl?"

She hesitated. "Well, I'm a secretary at a law firm."

The old woman dismissed this with a bony hand. "I mean, what are your financial expectations? What will you inherit?"

Sally couldn't hide the smile that came to her lips. She said, "I don't expect to inherit any money. None at all."

Aunt Vivian raised her eyebrows. Then she said, "That is too bad. A modest amount of inherited wealth is always a help."

"My family is not wealthy, though we always had enough," Sally told the old woman.

The gray head nodded sagely. "I understand. Forgive me for prying."

"It's quite all right," Sally said as the maid brought the bouquet of wildflowers into the room in a glass vase and set it on the table.

"Lovely," the old woman said. And she told the maid, "You can bring our tea and sandwiches now." Then she turned her attention to Sally again. "So your winning this prize, this trip to Holland, was a great boon to you."

"Yes."

"You must plan your life carefully," Aunt Vivian said. "Make the best of it. Look for a good marriage. You're not seriously interested in that painter who is doing my portrait, are you?"

Sally feared her blushing would give her secret away. "I think he's talented and very pleasant."

"I'll tell you a secret," the old woman said, leaning forward. "I fear my niece is in love with him. But we did discuss that last time perhaps. Anyway, she sees you as a possible rival. That's the reason for her shopping trip to Paris. To outdo you in dress if nothing else."

"I hope all you say isn't true," Sally protested.

"I believe it is," Aunt Vivian said. "And, frankly, I wouldn't consider a portrait artist a suitable match for either of you."

"He's more talented than many," Sally said.

"Even a talented artist rarely achieves any degree of true security," the old woman said. "Dorothy could afford him as a luxury. You surely can't."

Her cheeks still flaming, Sally said, "It is not my intention to marry for anything but love."

"Then be sure your love is wealthy," Aunt Vivian said as the maid arrived with the luncheon tray.

A little later, Sally sent up a trial balloon. "I believe Adam Bond is away from Amsterdam just now."

The old lady showed no surprise. "He often is absent from his studio. I've heard Dorothy complain about it. He's an artist—eccentric, unpredictable." She poured some more tea for Sally. "And please don't let yourself be caught in a contest with Dorothy over him."

Sally smiled faintly. "I certainly wouldn't want that."

"My niece will return with a new wardrobe, ready to turn the young man's head," Aunt Vivian said. "Let us hope that nothing comes of it. I'd blame myself in part for bringing her to Holland."

"You do enjoy it here," she said.

Aunt Vivian's stern face softened. "There are my memories. Faded memories of what might have been. And of more practical value, there is this fine arthritis specialist who has done wonders for me."

Sally smiled. "I can see you manage a nice balance between the past and present."

"Age brings a tiny premium in added wisdom," the old woman said with twinkle in her eyes.

"I'm sure it must," Sally agreed.

"When Dorothy returns, I'm going to encourage her to see you more often while you're in Amsterdam," the old woman said. "She has few true friends and none that I've met whom I'd judge as sensible as you."

Sally smiled. "I think that's overrating me."

"Not by the standards set by most of her friends," the old woman said. "She needs at least one sensible confidante who has a sound sense of values."

Sally said, "I'm afraid I'm not equipped to advise Dorothy what to do in her world."

"That's why I see you as being most valuable. You see things from the outside. You're objective. A friendship formed here could continue when we all return to New York."

"I do hope we can always be friends," Sally said politely. She noticed the old woman looked pale and suddenly tired, so she added, "I really must go now."

Aunt Vivian nodded. "Of course! And I shall have my afternoon nap. Do think about what I said."

"I will," Sally said, rising. "And thank you for everything."

"No thanks required," the old woman said. "I often get lonely here by myself. Remember what I told you."

"Yes," she said.

"I'll have Dorothy get in touch with you when she gets back," she said.

"Very well," Sally said. A few minutes later the maid showed her out.

As Sally walked back to her hotel, she was busily thinking of Adam and the Lanes. When she reached the Bergen House, she almost bumped into someone. Someone called Adam Bond.

When she found her voice, it sounded small and thin. She said, "So you've finally returned!"

He nodded soberly. "I guess you were trying to reach me."

"Wouldn't you expect that?" she asked.

"Yes. I just saw my uncle at the diamond shop. He told me you and some guy came looking for me."

"That's right. I was terribly worried." She was aware that Jacob Schok and everyone else in the tiny lobby were watching them and listening to all they said. So she suggested, "Let's go out and talk somewhere else."

"We can walk down by the docks," he suggested. "It will be cooler there. Always a little breeze."

As they headed for the docks, he said, "I had a rush call to go to Antwerp. A business matter, which I couldn't explain to you. I thought I'd only be gone overnight and be back shortly. But I was caught up in a series of problems and couldn't get back until today."

She said, "I wouldn't have given it a thought

if it had only been overnight. But you've been gone for several days and nights."

"I apologize."

Sally glanced up at him. "Did it have to do with your painting?"

"In a way," he said, without offering any other explanation.

She thought this rather odd. So she said, "It's something you don't want to discuss with me."

"That is correct," he said shortly.

Sally felt almost a physical hurt at this reply. But she stopped questioning him. Soon they had reached the docks and stood together on one of the deserted wharves. Adam looked very handsome with the breeze ruffling his blond hair.

She gazed out at a distant freighter riding at anchor. "I've just had lunch with Vivian Lane."

He showed interest. "What did they have to say?"

"Dorothy wasn't there."

"No?" he said.

"No," she said wryly. "She's off in Paris on a shopping trip. Her aunt thinks she's buying clothes to impress you with."

Adam showed disbelief. "You have to be joking."

"Not at all," Sally said. "I warned you Dorothy felt you were her property. She's only waiting for the right moment to claim you."

"You know better," he said soberly. "I told you my feelings the night before I had to go away."

She said, "Don't think it's anything I was apt to forget. You said you wanted to marry me."

"I do." He came close to her and was about to take her in his arms.

Sally stepped back a little and placed a hand forward to keep him at bay. "You remember we discussed some conditions. One of them being that you must tell Dorothy at once about us."

Adam hesitated. "Yes, I know I did agree to that."

"She'll be home shortly. You'll soon have a chance to see her," Sally said.

His handsome face took on a stubborn look. "About that," he said, "I had some time to think about it while I was away. And I'm not sure I should say anything to her just yet after all."

She was shocked by this. "You're not sure?" she echoed.

"That's right," he said evenly. "I have to finish her aunt's portrait and get the business of that settled. If Dorothy reacts badly to hearing about us, it could make it awkward. I think I'll wait until the transaction is completed."

"I see," she said with some irony. "You made

good use of your time while you were away."

"I hope so," he said. "I want to do what's best for all of us."

Sally moved away from him, her eyes on the freighter once more. "And you expect me to go along with this decision?"

"I know you're a reasonable person, Sally," he said.

"I don't think you really know me at all," was her opinion.

"Before I went away, I spoke to you of trust. And that you should trust me," he said urgently. "I think this is a time for you to prove such trust."

She looked up at him with a sad smile. "How can you expect me to trust you while you're asking me to join with you in cheating others?"

"Not cheating!" he said with a hint of upset. "Using a little discretion."

"So now we're talking about discretion," she said. "All right, let's be discreet! Completely! As far as I'm concerned, you've made no promises, nor have I! We'll start again, fresh."

He showed uneasiness. "But you know I am in love with you!"

"I cannot discreetly indulge myself in that at the moment," Sally told him. "That's part of what we've lost."

He stood with his fists clenched at his sides. "I'll soon have the painting done. We can halt the charade then. Just be patient."

"I'm going back to enjoying my holiday and not worrying about you," Sally told him. "What happens in the future, happens in the future."

He stared at her in disbelief. "I can't believe you are talking to me in this manner!"

Her smile was mocking. "By the way, I think I should tell you I've had another proposal while you were away."

Adam reacted sharply, staring at her in a state of shock, unable to reply. She turned and walked back toward the street, leaving him standing on the wharf alone.

Her throat was tight and her heart pounding. Her smile had concealed the deep pain she'd felt. Now that she was alone, it surged through her. Adam's betrayal of her love— and she could only think of it as that—left her at a complete loss.

She walked quickly, her thoughts in a turmoil. Probably Frank had been right. She'd been too hasty in taking Adam Bond seriously. Yet deep down she knew her feelings had been sincere, and she'd also felt he was in love with her. It had been a mistake, though, even if she hated to admit it.

Reaching the hotel, she stepped out of the sunlight, her mind still confused. Then old Jacob Schok came over to her and with a smile bowed.

"It is your day for visitors," he said. "The other young man was here."

She stared at him. "Oh?"

"Yes," the old man said. "I told him you'd gone out with another gentleman. And he said, if you came back anytime soon, you could find him in the coffee shop next door."

"Thank you," she murmured. And still in a state of agitation, she went back out again and down to the coffee shop. She discovered Frank seated on a stool.

He patted the stool next to him and said, "I've been saving this for you. And by the way, it isn't every day that the young lady I've asked to be my wife stands me up for another gent."

CHAPTER TWELVE

Sally sat down on the stool and warned him, "It isn't my good afternoon for jokes."

Frank registered amazement. "I'll have you know I wasn't joking. I made a most serious statement. I'm sure you recall the important question I put to you last night."

"And the spirit in which it was offered," she said knowingly. "I'll not hold you to anything you may have said."

"I'm not sure I can accept your generosity," the young writer teased her. "What I must know at the moment, to assuage my hurt pride, is who the man was you were out with just now."

She gave him a bleak look. "Adam Bond. He's back."

"Then why so gloomy? I'd expect you to be shouting with joy, considering the laments I was hearing about his unexpected absence."

"It's rather complicated."

"With you, it always is," Frank said. "Most young women would welcome him back and that would be that. You have to keep on making a fuss about it."

Her eyes met Frank's and she said, "I'm beginning to believe a lot of the things you said were right."

"I've always insisted I'm a fountain of wisdom," Frank said. "To which of my sayings do you refer?"

"About my falling in love with Adam too quickly. Not knowing enough about him."

The young writer said, "Well, that's just basic stuff. Good sense, if you follow me."

"I wish I had followed you earlier," she sighed. "At any rate, I'm not even sure Adam and I are still friends anymore."

He considered this with exaggerated interest and then said, "Point one, don't expect this news to overwhelm me with sadness. Point two, what has caused this sudden rift between you two?"

"Several things."

"He revealed his absence had to do with

some kind of romantic activity?" Frank suggested.

"No."

"What did take him away so suddenly?"

"He wouldn't tell me," she admitted. "He did say it had to do with some art business. That's all. He went on a lot of nonsense about my having trust in him."

Frank said, "In other words, he wasn't too helpful."

"He was not," she agreed. "He didn't seem to care that I worried myself sick about him. On top of all that, he's still trying to cater to Dorothy and her aunt. Give Dorothy wrong ideas."

"About his interest in her?"

"Yes. I didn't think he'd be guilty of such a thing," she said brokenly. "But now I have to face it."

"He's known this Lane girl longer than he has you," Frank said.

"I know," she sighed. "I just want to forget the whole business. I want to enjoy the rest of my vacation and go back to New York without ever thinking of Adam Bond again."

Frank beamed at her. "Now I call that showing good sense. You're giving me the kind of story I can do full justice to."

"All you care about is that magazine story," she accused him. "You're a nice letdown as well!"

"Stop!" he ordered her and touched her arm.

"I only ask that you give me a chance to redeem myself."

"That," she said, giving him a stony glance, "will take a good deal of doing!"

She didn't realize it then, but it was the beginning of a new and very good time for her in Amsterdam. Frank Kincaide knew the old city well and he gave almost his full time to taking Sally around, keeping her busy, and making sure she was enjoying her vacation.

The days passed very quickly. Soon it would be back to New York, with all the excitement and romance of Amsterdam behind her. She tried not to think about Adam Bond and had ignored several messages and phone calls from him. But every so often, she remembered the whirlwind romance they'd had and shed some secret tears. Most of the time, Frank kept her too occupied for silent sorrow and she found herself growing to like the young writer more and more.

In contrast to Adam, Frank was hardly ever serious. He gave Sally special attention without pressing her to make any pledge to him. It seemed that every night he found some new place to dine or dance, or some exciting event to attend.

When she'd decided he'd exhausted all the different places, he asked her, "How would you like to go ice-skating?"

She laughed. "In June?"

"It's the very best time," he assured her.

"And I have the place. Have you heard of the Silver Skates Cafe?"

"No! What is it?"

"A fine dining room and cabaret with a wonderful ice-skating act. And when the show is over, the patrons can rent skates and go on the ice rather than dancing."

"I don't believe there is such a place!"

"Have I ever been wrong before?"

She laughed. "No. But I'll really be impressed if you come up with an ice-skating cabaret!"

He gave her a wise look. "Tonight is the night!"

So at eight o'clock that evening she was introduced to the Silver Skates Cafe. The waiters were dressed in white dinner jackets and most efficient. Everything suggested the place had to be expensive.

Frank leaned across the table to tell her, "This is chiefly for rich tourists and wealthy locals."

"Can you afford it?" Sally worried.

He laughed. "I'm doing a story on the place, so I get to put it all on an expense account."

"I'm beginning to see the benefits of being a roving member of the press," Sally said.

"Speaking of things special," he said, "you do me credit in that red dress."

"And you look quite handsome in the impeccable dark suit."

The waiter brought them menus and Frank

told her, "After the dinner is served, there's a half-hour show. Then the ice is available to anyone."

Sally shook her head. "I'm not sure I want to try."

Frank told her, "There's lots of time for you to decide."

They ordered from the imposing menu and then sat back to enjoy the meal.

By the time dessert arrived, Sally was full. "The pastries look lovely, but can I manage any room for anything more?"

"Have a taste, anyway," Frank urged. "It will finish off your dinner."

At about that time the lights were dimmed and a half-dozen colorfully dressed male and female skaters appeared. To the accompaniment of four musicians, they went through a fast and clever show in whirlwind fashion.

The show ended and an announcement was made that skates were available. Everyone was invited on the ice. Frank finally persuaded a hesitant Sally to skate with him. Soon they were fitted with skates and cautiously making their way around the circular rink.

Sally turned to Frank, smiling. "It is fun! I'm glad I tried it!"

"I thought you would be glad," he said.

She looked ahead again and almost lost her balance on the ice. Coming toward them, also

on skates, were Dorothy in a lovely green outfit and Adam in a dark suit.

Dorothy saw Sally and waved. "Let's meet
on the next time around."

Adam looked grim and embarrassed in contrast to the auburn-haired girl's friendliness.

"Who was that?" Frank wanted to know.

"Adam and that Dorothy Lane girl, the rich
one," Sally said. "She wants us to meet when
we pass next time."

Frank looked amused. "Do you want to?"

"I guess we'll have to," she stammered.
"Dorothy is making all the overtures."

They skated over to the side and a moment
later Dorothy and Adam came gliding over to
them. Sally quickly made introductions all
around.

Dorothy turned on all her charm for Frank,
saying, "So you are the mysterious writer
we've been hearing so much about."

"Not all that mysterious," Frank protested.
Sally could see he was sizing the other two
up.

Adam had said little more than hello.

Dorothy turned to Sally and told her, "I
haven't been able to reach you since my trip
to Paris. I have so many new things. And Aunt
Vivian is very much impressed by you and
thinks we two should become friends."

"She's very nice," Sally said. "But I'll only
be in Amsterdam a short time longer."

"But you will be in New York," Dorothy said. "And that is where Aunt Vivian and I are most of the time."

Frank, meanwhile, spoke to Adam about his painting.

Dorothy turned to Adam, smiling, and suggested, "Why don't we end the evening by all going to your studio? You can show Frank the painting of Aunt Vivian you've just completed and the other ones."

Adam showed hesitation in accepting the idea. He said, "I'm not certain they would be interested."

"We would," Frank said. "At least that's my feeling. I'm sure Sally agrees even though she's seen your stuff before."

Sally managed a stifled, "Yes."

Dorothy took over in her usual way. "Then it's all settled. Do you have a car, Frank?"

"In the parking lot," he said. "Sally knows the address so she can co-pilot me."

"We'll meet you there!" Dorothy said with shrill delight. "Isn't this fun?"

As Frank led Sally off the ice, he said in a low voice, "It isn't fun at all if I measure it by your face and Adam's. You both looked like condemned people."

"A stupid idea," Sally said bitterly. "And you could have helped by not showing all that interest in his work."

"The interest is genuine," Frank pointed out. "I'd also like to know this paragon of men better. He's not all that friendly."

"He's caught in an awkward spot," she said. "I'm glad you were here with me. Let Adam see I'm not sitting in some corner being miserable."

Frank eyed her with interest as they went out to the parking lot. "So that is my mission in life. Being a decoration for you."

Dorothy and Adam arrived at the studio a few minutes before Sally and Frank joined them. Dorothy was fussing about in the kitchen.

When they appeared, she came out to greet them. "I'm glad you were able to find your way. I'll get some coffee in a moment."

"Don't bother for us," Frank said.

The auburn-haired girl smiled for his benefit. "It's no bother at all." And to Adam, who was standing by dejectedly, she added, "Do show them Aunt Vivian's portrait, dear."

Meekly Adam went over and removed a white cloth drape from the large study of Vivian Lane. Sally had not seen it for some time and she was impressed at the detail and amount of color he'd been able to add to the painting.

"It's very good!" she said, meaning it.

"Thanks," Adam said quietly.

"I like it," Frank agreed. "But I like this one just as well." He was indicating a smaller study of Sally. He asked, "What do you want for it?"

"It's not for sale," Adam said stiffly.

Sally, who had not sat for the study nor seen it before, tried to cover her confusion by asking, "Are you taking these to New York?"

"I'm shipping some ahead shortly," he told her. "I'll leave a few pieces with dealers here."

Dorothy linked her arm in Adam's in a possessive fashion and told them, "I'm going to work hard when Adam returns to New York to see he meets the right people and gets good commissions. My aunt's portrait can be only a beginning."

Frank looked amused. "I guess times don't change that much for artists. They still need their patrons."

Dorothy looked at him as he said this, with an expression that suggested she didn't know whether to be flattered or annoyed. In the end she compromised by saying, "You can come to the kitchen and help me with the coffee." And she led him off without giving him a chance to object.

Sally and Adam were left alone at the end of the big gallery away from the kitchen. He looked at her sadly and she glanced down to avoid his eyes. Dorothy could be heard chatting in the kitchen, with Frank occasionally getting in a word. The silence between Sally and Adam was thunderous.

"I haven't changed my mind about anything," he finally said in a low voice.

"Really?" Sally tried to sound casual.

"I love you and I know that you love me," he went on. "Why haven't you answered my calls?"

"I've been busy."

"With *him?*"

She looked up fiercely. "Frank is a very nice person. I admire his integrity."

Adam stepped closer to her. "You used to admire mine."

"Did I?"

He reached out to take her in his arms, saying, "Sally, let's not waste precious time battling each other!"

He undoubtedly would have tried to embrace her if Dorothy and Frank hadn't arrived at that precise moment with the coffee. Adam turned away quickly and Sally busied herself helping Dorothy with the cups and a tray of cakes.

Somehow Sally had the feeling that Dorothy had seen enough to guess that Adam had been trying to patch things up with her. The auburn-haired girl handled the situation well, but Sally thought she was a little too tense.

Dorothy turned her attention to Frank, saying, "I think it is wonderful of you to take Sally under your wing and show her the city."

"Believe me, the pleasure has been mine," Frank said. "And it is helping me with a magazine story I'm doing on Americans in Amsterdam."

"I gather the magazine is paying all the bills," Dorothy said.

"No. Most of our dates are our own affair," Frank said. "Nothing to do with the airline or the magazine."

"How mean of them!" Dorothy said, playing out her role. And to Sally, she said, "I'll call you at your hotel tomorrow. As I remember, I have to leave the message at the desk."

"Correct," she said. "No room phones."

"Well, that doesn't discourage me." The auburn-haired girl smiled sweetly. "I think we ought to know each other better."

Frank glanced at his watch. "And I say it is time for us to be on our way. I have to get a story off early in the morning to New York."

"You must tell me more about it some time," Dorothy said. "I have always been on my guard with magazine people. It's nice to meet someone in the business on a personal basis."

Frank smiled. "I promise I will never betray you." And they said their good nights and made their way from the studio.

In the car Frank gave Sally a wise glance and said, "Was that some tricky situation!"

"What do you mean?"

"That moment when we came in and found you and Adam about to fall into each other's arms!"

She frowned. "Did it honestly look like that?"

"It sure did," he told her. "And you noticed how nervous Dorothy was afterward. How nasty she became."

"That's her usual way," Sally said.

Frank started the car. "Well, she changed the moment she saw you two staring into each other's eyes like a couple of moon-struck young lovers."

"We're anything but that!"

"Say, you were giving a good imitation," he told her.

"Nothing has changed," she said bitterly. "I told him that."

"The question is, does he believe it?"

"He should. You saw the way they are together. Dorothy talks and acts as if they were already married."

Frank smiled. "I say she's running frightened."

"Never!"

"I do. She's still worried about you. That's why she's decided to make you more her friend. Another way of disarming you."

Sally gave him a reproachful glance. "I think you're reading too much into all this."

"Wait and see."

"Adam has sold out to Dorothy and her aunt. I can't think why Dorothy should worry about me."

When they reached the door of her hotel, they remained seated in the car for a little.

She asked Frank, "You've met them both. What do you think of them?"

He smiled. "Routine types. I wouldn't give them a second look if you weren't involved."

"Please," she said, placing a hand on his. "I

really want to know your opinion of them."

Frank sighed. "Well, he's talented. No denying that."

"It is so true!" she said, pleased by this.

The young writer eyed her bleakly. "But you're not going to like the rest of what I have to say about him. I think he's used to living off wealthy clients and he's not all that bright aside from his artistic talent."

Her eyes blazed. "Those are terrible things to say!"

"You asked me," he reminded her.

She sat back and then asked, "What about Dorothy?"

"Beautiful, smart, and totally without ethics. She sees Adam Bond as a big talent who will have his name in tall letters, yet realizes he is someone who can be manipulated. And she intends to do that to her own advantage."

"You think she expects to marry him?"

"Probably."

Sally gave him a pleading look. "Why does he keep on saying he loves only me?"

Frank grimaced. "It could be a bad habit!"

"Now you're making fun of me again," she said unhappily. "I felt I could at least count on you."

Frank reached out and circled his arm around her and, in a different tone, said, "That is the only thing you can be sure of. That you can count on me." And he drew her to him so that their lips met. His kiss was long, warm, and tender.

When he released her, he offered her a sad smile as he said, "That's my statement, Inspector. The rest you'll have to figure out for yourself."

CHAPTER THIRTEEN

Going bicycle riding in the park had been Dorothy's idea. She had managed to reach Sally a few mornings later on a fine day and broach the project. Sally's first reaction was to try to avoid the auburn-haired girl, but Dorothy seemed so genuinely friendly and anxious for an afternoon's sport that she agreed.

They rented the bicycles in the park and made their way along one of the paths. It was an enchanted world of its own, and Sally found herself enjoying it thoroughly. Dorothy was a stronger cyclist than she, so Dorothy led the way. After some time, they found a flat, grassy knoll with a lovely view. They put down their bikes and stretched out on the grass in the warm sun.

"I shall hate to leave," Sally admitted as she gazed at the scene before her.

"I could stay on," Dorothy said. "But I won't. Aunt Vivian is restless to get to her summer place in Maine."

Sally gave the other girl a rueful smile. "Maine doesn't sound so bad. I'll be pounding back and forth to work on steamy Manhattan streets."

Dorothy sat up and clasped her hands around her jean-clad knees. "You know, I think Adam Bond is in love with you."

Sally gave her an astonished look. "Why do you say that?"

The auburn-haired girl smiled grimly. "I have several reasons. The way you two were looking at each other when I came into the studio that night. And the portrait he did of you."

"I didn't sit for it," Sally told her. "He must have done it from memory or from some snapshot."

Dorothy said, "However he did it, you were in his mind."

Sally found this impossible to deny. So she lamely suggested, "I don't think it has any importance at all."

"Don't think I'll let you have him."

"There's no contest," Sally said. "I'd like us to be friends and the best way to do that is not discuss Adam at all."

Dorothy offered one of her arrogant smiles. "He was lost as soon as he accepted the commission to do Aunt Vivian's portrait. She'll be taking it and paying for it in a few days. And there will be no turning back for him."

"He has talent. I wish him success," Sally said.

"You'd really be bad for him," Dorothy went on. "You have nothing financially to offer. You haven't even any influential friends."

"And you have both."

"I like to think so," Dorothy said. "Adam doesn't realize what I can do for him."

"Why don't you try to explain?"

"I don't think it's the right moment," the other girl said. "Especially since he still has this odd crush on you."

"I haven't seen him lately, only the other night when he was with you," Sally said.

"I know," Dorothy said, giving her a searching glance. "Have you counted the hours?"

She blushed. "I hope not."

Dorothy persisted, "I mean, how much in love with him are you?"

"I'd rather not discuss it."

"You really don't know, is my guess."

Sally shrugged. "You could be close to the truth."

"I know where I stand," Dorothy bragged. "I'm not confused by any nonsense of love. I care for him, naturally, but mostly I'm ambitious for him. I want to see him famous."

Sally said, "And you think that's enough?"

"It should be more than enough," Dorothy said smugly. "Better than love and poverty, with his talent wasting away for lack of recognition."

Sally stared at the auburn-haired girl and quietly said, "The frightening thing is you are convincing. I can see the logic of what you're saying. You have the strength, the cunning, and the clarity of mind to do all you've said."

"Thanks," Dorothy said, watching her closely.

Sally stood up, hands on her hips. With a wry smile, she told the other girl, "Forgive me if I say that without you truly caring, it isn't enough."

The auburn-haired girl smiled slowly. "I really don't need your opinion."

Sally replied, "I think what you mean to say is that you don't want it."

Dorothy jumped up. "That will do. So let's complete the trail and then go back."

It was the finish of any frank discussion between them. When they parted, they were polite and vaguely agreed to meet again.

That evening Sally and Frank had dinner together at a small cafe. She told him about her afternoon with Dorothy. The young writer listened with his usual interest.

Studying her seriously across the table, he

asked, "You were completely honest with her, weren't you?"

"As honest as I dared be."

"You do think she'd be a disaster for him?"

"Yes," Sally said.

"You may not be right in that," Frank warned her. "Some men I know are completely happy with an efficient wife to manage them and a modest amount of recognition for their work."

"It would destroy Adam's talent."

"I wonder," Frank said. "At least Dorothy has put you on the alert. She's out to capture our artist friend."

"I also let her know I'm not a rival."

"I don't believe it," Frank said. "And, I'd be willing to bet, neither does she."

She sighed. "Well, only a few days to New York. Then it will all be memories."

"Very flattering to me," he said.

She gave him a warm smile and reached out to touch his hand. "You'll be a good memory."

"Not exactly my ambition," he told her. "I'd much rather go on playing an active role. By the way, I tried to get in touch with Adam today and he wasn't at his studio."

She nodded. "Dorothy mentioned that. She said he had to go to Berlin."

"He seems to have a lot of business out of town."

Sally explained, "He's acted as consultant

to an art gallery there. He appraises old paintings before their auctions."

Frank nodded. "So I've heard. I'm working on a new assignment and I hope he may be able to help me with it."

"What sort of assignment?"

The young writer smiled. "Very hush-hush at present. I'll tell you when I can."

"And you think Adam might be able to supply some information?" she asked.

"Yes. It does seem that he might." Frank paused. "You've met some of his friends, I suppose."

"Not really," she said. "I did have dinner with his uncle. You also met him."

"I mean aside from his uncle."

"I've seen him with a dealer. But he didn't introduce him to me. Mostly they talked in Dutch. He didn't appear anxious to have me know the man, so I assume they weren't close."

"Interesting," Frank said. "If you can think of anything else, tell me."

She stared at him. "I don't understand. Is there something wrong? Is Adam mixed up in anything?"

"I didn't say that," he told her.

"But there's something in your manner," she said. "I'm not sure that I like it."

He laughed. "My professional routine of questioning. I've never used it on you before. Just forget I said anything."

She was still worried. She said, "Adam

would never talk to me about his absences.
All I know I've heard from other people."

"Didn't you think that strange?"

"It bothered me," she admitted. "But he
asked me to trust him and vowed he was doing
nothing wrong. So I believed him."

Frank smiled. "Then that's where we'd best
leave it."

He saw her home. After he left, as she lay
trying to sleep, his questions nagged her. Also,
the fact that Adam was off to Berlin on some
mission troubled her. From the start she'd had
an odd premonition that there might be more
to these excursions than she knew. Now Frank
Kincaide's questions brought the problem in
focus. It made her realize there was much
about Adam she had yet to learn.

She doubted that Dorothy knew any more.
But Dorothy wasn't one to torture herself with
troublesome questions. She was more likely
to smoothly pass them over and concentrate
on the positive. Perhaps this would also be the
best way for her. Sally fell asleep with her
mind still in a whirl.

The rain she woke up to the following morning did not improve her mood. She had no
plans for the day. It was close to the end of
her stay and so she'd exhausted most of the
tourist activities. She went out for breakfast
and, when she came back, the old elevator
man was waiting for her with a slip of paper
in his hand.

"Message for you, miss," Jacob Schok said.

"Thank you, Jacob," Sally replied, taking the paper and reading the message written in the old man's cramped hand. "Meet me at the Royal Amsterdam Hotel restaurant for lunch. Twelve-thirty, sharp—Vivian Lane."

Sally was punctual, and the headwaiter quickly took her to Vivian Lane's table after she'd checked her raincoat and umbrella.

"You managed, my dear girl," the old woman said. "What a terror this dripping city is. My limousine was held up several times by great floods in the streets."

Sally allowed the headwaiter to help her to her seat opposite the older woman. She said, "I walked. It wasn't far, but it is a torrential downpour."

"Never mind," Dorothy's aunt said. "We are safely here. And Dorothy is at her beautician's for the morning, or more properly most of the day. I knew it was her day to go. That is why I set up this meeting with you."

"I see," Sally said, wondering what the old woman had in mind.

"I'm much alarmed," Vivian Lane said grimly.

"About what?"

"I believe my niece is on the verge of marrying that young artist." The lined pale face showed strain.

"Do you so object to the match?"

"Yes. And you know my reasons. I thought

you and he were supposed to be in love. What happened?"

Sally smiled ruefully. "I'm not sure I can tell you. Just a number of things."

"Dorothy is already planning their future."

"I'm not surprised," Sally said.

The old blue eyes were fixed on her. "You're taking it calmly enough."

"Yes," she said quietly.

"I rather expected you to battle Dorothy for your man," Aunt Vivian told her.

"I want Adam to be happy."

"He never will with my niece. I'd give the marriage one year, maybe two. Then she'll discard him for a new toy. I'm sorry I ever had him do my portrait. That was the start of it all."

"But he did such a magnificent study of you!"

The old woman nodded grimly. "I'm aware of that. I've put off taking delivery as long as possible. I'm fearful that when I do, he and Dorothy will take it as a cue to announce their plans to marry."

"You haven't paid him yet?"

"No. I wish I could find some excuse for not taking it," the old woman grumbled. "But, as you say, it is a perfectly good work of art."

Sally asked, "What does Dorothy think of Adam being so secretive about his personal life. Especially about his sudden mysterious trips out of the city?"

"I've heard her complain about them, but I

don't think she ever discussed this with him.
She's not able to think of anything now but of
taking him from you."

Sally said, "I've made it easy for her."

"I can't understand it," Aunt Vivian said.
"I hoped I might convince you to try and get
your man back."

"No chance," she said. "Adam does as he
likes."

Aunt Vivian sat back with a sigh. "Well, no
need to let it ruin our luncheon. We shall order
a lot of rich and expensive dishes."

An hour later Sally escorted the old woman
out to her waiting limousine. She leaned out
the back window after the chauffeur had
helped her inside.

She told Sally, "I think I know your state of
mind. You're terribly confused. But from my
small observation, I'd say you would be a lot
better for that artist than Dorothy. She'll destroy him!"

Sally nodded as the old woman sat back in
the big black car and ordered the limousine
to drive off. Vivian Lane had offered to take
Sally to her hotel, but she had declined the
offer. The rain had ended and she felt like
walking a while in the fresh air.

She found herself on one of the busy shopping streets. And as she came to a window
filled with lovely diamond displays, she read
the name, Berkhim Brothers, on the shop's
window in gold lettering. She was instantly

reminded of Adam's uncle. He had told her
this was where he worked and that it would
be the best place to contact him.

A moment later, she was on her way inside.
She didn't know what she was going to say,
but she felt seeing the man and talking to him
might in some fashion ease her tension.

The thin, gray-haired male clerk bowed to
Sally as she entered the store.

She told him, "I'm an American. A friend
of mine is one of your diamond cutters."

The man showed polite interest. "Indeed. He
would be in the shop upstairs."

"His name is Theo Muller," she said. "May
I go up and speak with him?"

The clerk hesitated and said, "Let me first
phone the work room and see if he is there."
And he went behind the counter to a house
phone.

Sally was relieved that the store remained
empty. The clerk conducted a conversation over
the house phone in a low voice. Once he gave
her a peculiar glance over his shoulder; then
he said something into the phone again and
hung up.

He now returned to Sally with a masked
expression on his lined face and said, "I regret
we have no Theo Muller employed here."

She gasped. It was happening again. "But
you must have," she insisted.

"I am sorry, miss," the man replied.

"There has to be some mistake," Sally said,

grasping for an explanation. "He could be using a different name here, he sometimes does that."

The clerk shook his head. "We would know his true identity if he were employed in our workshop. You must have become confused in the name of the dealer."

She saw by the stolid face and manner of the clerk she would get no further help from him. Her only alternative was to retreat as gracefully as she could. She thanked him politely and hurriedly made her exit.

Back on the busy street, Sally felt more lost than ever. The benign Theo Muller was certainly evasive. There had to be some strange explanation for the behavior of Adam's uncle. She began to feel the man wasn't his uncle at all but some kind of associate.

Now the mysterious comments Frank had made about the young artist came back to her. She hurried back to her hotel and called Frank's office at Global.

When he answered, she told him, "I need to see you."

At the other end of the phone, Frank said, "You sound upset."

"I am," she said. "Can you come straight here?"

"That urgent?"

"Yes!"

"Give me twenty minutes," he said.

"I'll be waiting for you in the lobby," she told him."

Frank arrived before the twenty minutes were up and went to the corner of the lobby where she'd seated herself. He said, "What has happened?"

"Let's stroll to the square," she said, not wanting to talk about it in the lobby with so many to overhear her.

When they reached the street, he gave her a troubled glance, saying, "You look pale and ill."

She smiled sourly. "I've had another weird experience." And she told him about visiting the diamond shop.

Frank heard her out, then said, "I'm not surprised."

She looked at him wide-eyed. "You're not?"

"No," he said as they waited by the curb before crossing the street. "I was almost certain he was lying to us that night."

"Why didn't you say so?" she asked.

He shrugged and took her by the arm to see her across when the light changed. "I didn't want to upset you unless I was sure about him. I wasn't then."

"But you are now?"

"Reasonably," he said as they stood in the quieter area of the square.

"If he's not Adam's uncle, who is he?" she worried.

"That's an interesting question."

"And why did Adam have me meet him in the first place?" Sally said, her bafflement showing in her eyes.

"Another equally interesting question," the young writer said with cryptic cheerfulness.

Exasperated, she pulled at his arm and cried, "Don't give me all those meaningless statements. Tell me what I want to know."

Frank apologized, "Sorry!"

"You should be," she said angrily. "Now go on."

"You've been duped."

"By Adam?"

"I'm very much afraid so," the young writer said. "From all I've been able to discover, your artist friend is involved in some sort of shady business."

"I can't believe it!" she protested.

Frank gave her a knowing look. "Think of all those sudden trips away."

"They had something to do with it?"

"Yes. And probably so did the man he introduced as his uncle," Frank said.

"You're saying he's mixed up in something criminal?" she asked in disbelief.

"Based on the little I've discovered, yes," Frank said. "I told you I was working on a special story. He happens to be part of it."

"Surely, you can tell me what it's all about."

He shook his head. "I'm afraid my arrangement with the Dutch police forbids my talking to anyone at this time."

She stared at him, stunned. "The Dutch police!"

"I'm sorry, Sally," he said, his hand on her arm. "You'll just have to wait a little more."

CHAPTER FOURTEEN

The next morning when Sally went down to the lobby of the small hotel, the clerk in charge had another phoned message for her.

The young man passed it to her and said, "It came about a half hour ago."

"Thank you," she said. The message was short but urgent: "Must see you at once. Strange developments concerning Adam Bond." The caller was Vivian Lane.

Sally stuffed the note in the pocket of her jacket and with a sigh made her way out to the street and the small cafe where she always had her morning meal.

Over her coffee, she tried to get the confused

events straight in her mind. Frank's revelation that Adam was in some way afoul of the police had stunned her. Now it seemed that through some source Vivian and Dorothy Lane had also had a report on the young man and wished to compare notes with her.

It placed her in a difficult position. Through all the twists of recent weeks, she had remained a staunch admirer of Adam. She in no way wished to be disloyal to him. If the appeal had come only from Dorothy, she would have ignored it, but she did not like to ignore a message from the old woman.

Sally decided it would be best for her to go see Dorothy and her aunt, yet be discreet in offering any opinions. In fairness to Adam, they did not know what he might be accused of, or whether he could be innocent. Frank had refused to give her any details.

Before she left for the hotel where the Lanes had their suite, she tried to contact Frank on the phone. But he was not in his office and the secretary did not know when he'd be back. So Sally found a taxi and made her way to the Lanes' hotel.

The tired-looking maid opened the door for Sally and recognized her. "Good morning, miss," the woman said.

"Is Miss Vivian Lane in?" she asked.

The woman nodded. "Yes. They are both in the sitting room waiting for you, miss."

Sally thanked her and entered the familiar

room. Dorothy, in a purple dressing gown, was looking out the big window disconsolately, while her Aunt Vivian sat very erect in her usual high-backed chair.

The old woman greeted Sally warmly, saying, "How good of you to come."

"I felt it might be urgent," Sally said.

Dorothy turned from the window and glared at her. "It surely is urgent! It's more than that! It's incredible!"

Aunt Vivian gave her niece a look of reproach. "That sort of frantic talk will get us nowhere," she warned. And to Sally, she said, "Have you heard any dark rumors about Adam Bond?"

Sally knew she must be frank with them and still try to be fair to Adam. She said, "My friend, Frank Kincaide, the writer, knows something about Adam. He wasn't able to tell me what. But he did suggest his informant was the Dutch police."

"They've been here!" Dorothy exclaimed. "The police have actually been here questioning us."

Aunt Vivian asked Sally, "Have the police visited you?"

"No," she said.

Dorothy began to pace back and forth and gesticulate. "I can't think why we should have been subjected to the embarrassment."

Sally asked, "What did they seem to want?"

The old woman scowled. "It's hard for us to

say. They wanted to know how we'd met the young man. Also, whether I had commissioned him to do my portrait and whether I had paid him. I said that I hadn't and didn't intend to do so until I received the portrait here."

Dorothy said angrily, "From what they said, he's in some sort of con game. They appeared to feel we might be targets of it. How could he do this to us?"

Sally said, "He hasn't really done anything to you. He can't help the police investigating him. It's too bad they bothered you, but that doesn't mean he's guilty of anything."

"I think he is," Dorothy shot back. "And I can't forgive myself for falling in love with him."

Her Aunt Vivian glared at her. "I say you never did do that. You just decided to take him over as a new diversion!"

"That's not so!" Dorothy protested. "He gave me the impression he loved me and I was ready to give him my heart. And all the time he's a cheap crook!"

Sally found herself becoming angry. She said, "I can't let you call him that without proof," she said. "You're being cowardly and unfair."

Dorothy smiled at her nastily. "Look, who's talking. You were head-over-heels in love with him. You'd have married him in a minute if he'd asked you."

Sally hesitated for a moment before she quietly replied, "As a matter of fact, he did ask me."

The effect on Dorothy was instant. Anger painted red blotches on her cheeks and she cried, "I don't believe it! You're making it up!"

'I'm telling you the truth," Sally said.

"Then why didn't you marry him? You've been frightened enough that I would!" Dorothy shrilled.

Aunt Vivian said, "I will not tolerate this behavior! If we cannot talk in a civilized, sensible manner, we'd better not discuss the matter at all."

"That suits me!" Dorothy said, and she stalked out of the sitting room.

A moment later, you could hear the door of her room slam shut after her.

The old woman sat back with a sigh. "You have seen what I've had to contend with?"

"I'm sorry," Sally said. "I'm afraid my coming here has only made matters worse."

"Not at all," Dorothy's aunt told her. "I'd say your views were sane and fair. I admire you for not jumping to conclusions, as Dorothy seems to have done."

Sally said, "It would be so much easier if Adam were here and we could talk to him directly."

"He'll have to return sooner or later. Then we'll know," the old woman said. "I don't care about my niece's hysterical reaction. I asked him to paint my portrait and I will surely accept it and pay for it."

"I somehow feel it will all work out," Sally said. "I can't think what trouble he may have gotten himself into."

The old woman said, "The police were vague. They gave no real clues for their visit. They put their questions to us and answered none of ours."

Sally smiled ruefully. "It's a pathetic climax to my holiday here."

"I know. It is too bad."

"Part of gaining life experience," Sally said. "I'm sure I was in love with Adam. I still may be."

The old woman nodded. "One doesn't turn love off and on like a light switch unless you happen to be Dorothy."

"I'd better go back to my hotel," Sally said. "The police could be there looking for me."

"They could be," the old woman said. "How much longer do you have here?"

"Four days," she said. "It doesn't seem possible."

"Poor child!" Aunt Vivian said sympathetically. "And these should be your happiest days!"

"I only hope there's nothing about this that might make the police try to hold me here. I'm due back at my job."

"We must all join in protest if anything like that happens," the old woman said. "Let us keep in touch, so we'll know what is going on."

"I'll let you know anything I find out," Sally promised. "I hope Dorothy calms down a little."

"Don't worry about her," the old woman said. "She always does. It's a pity she's so shallow."

This time Vivian Lane insisted on showing Sally out herself. At the door, the old woman kissed her on the cheek and said, "Don't worry too much, my dear!"

Her gesture left Sally feeling better as she made her way to the street again. She had expected Dorothy to be difficult but not as bad as she had been. She was amazed at the little it took to confuse and upset the auburn-haired girl. Again she thought that Dorothy would make the worst sort of wife for anyone with Adam Bond's mild temperament.

Sally decided to walk rather than take a taxi. The day was sunny and warm, and she felt regrets at leaving the pleasant little land. And she worried about Adam. Stopping at a public phone booth, she tried Frank again at his office.

This time she reached him and told him about calling on the Lanes. She said, "They're very upset by the police questioning."

"I can imagine," he said. "You also have to expect it."

"No one has bothered me so far."

"They'll be talking with all Adam's friends

and associates," he said. "By the way, my latest tip is that Adam returned from Berlin late last night."

Her heart gave a small leap of joy. "Then he's here! We may be able to talk to him."

"I don't know about that," Frank said. "But the word is that he's back."

"If you hear anything more, please let me know. Leave word at the hotel desk," she urged him.

"I'll do better than that," he said warmly. "I'll come over and see you. I'd enjoy the excuse."

It was when she left the phone booth that the impulse hit her. She decided she would go to Adam's studio and see if he might be there. She rushed to the curb and hailed a passing taxi and gave him the address of the studio.

Five minutes later, she was standing before the downstairs door, feeling just a little nervous. She was going to press the buzzer when she noticed the door was slightly ajar. Since she knew her way in, she went ahead and up the steps to the studio. Voices came to her, voices speaking in Dutch.

She reached the studio and down at the end of it stood Adam and the older man he'd introduced to her as his uncle. Adam saw her at this same instant and took a step toward her; the older man remained where he was, staring at her with a bland expression.

Adam came up to her and exclaimed, "Sally!"

She managed a smile. "Hello, Adam, I see you have your elusive uncle with you today."

The tall, blond man looked guilty. "Sorry about that."

"I trusted you," she reminded him.

"I know," he said grimly. "I asked you to do that. Remember?"

"When you discussed it, I wasn't expecting the police to be involved," she said.

"I wanted to warn you. I couldn't."

"I'd like to know what is going on," Sally said. "I may tell you the police have been to Dorothy and her Aunt Vivian."

He groaned. "I hoped that wouldn't happen! I suppose the old girl is in a fine state!"

"Actually, no," Sally said. "It's Dorothy who had hysterics. She's furious at you, finished with you."

Adam grimaced. "Let's say she deserved to have hysterics!" And he turned to the older man and beckoned for him to join them. To her, he said, "This is the moment for an introduction."

She said dryly, "Not again! He never seems to be who he is, nor where he should be."

The old man chuckled at this. "I'm sorry, Miss Sheldon."

Adam said, "You were given his right name, but not his full title, this is Inspector Theo Muller. He's with a special division of the Dutch police. And that puppeteer you noticed is also a part of the special division."

Sally smiled at them. "Am I supposed to believe this?"

The inspector brought out a wallet and showed her his identification. "This time we are being frank with you," he said.

"I take it you're not Adam's uncle," she challenged him.

"I wish I were," the inspector said. "A talented man is Adam Bond. No, I played that role as part of our little game."

"What is your little game?" she asked.

Adam turned to the inspector. "Surely, there is no reason for silence any longer."

"There are still two or three to be rounded up," the older man reminded him. "But I'm sure we can trust Miss Sheldon to be discreet."

"Good!" Adam said. "It will be easier to explain if I show you something." And he went back to the other end of the studio, ransacked among some canvases piled against the wall, and then brought back a twenty-by-twenty-eight period painting of a park scene.

He held the nineteenth-century painting up for her to study as he asked, "Does it look familiar to you?"

She stared at it and frowned. "Yes, it does! It's rather famous, if I'm right. I saw it at one of the galleries."

Adam exchanged a triumphant look with the inspector and told her, "You have a good memory. It is a Kelzer, and was painted in 1891."

"Of course, a Kelzer! You can tell by the style," she said, admiring the color and sharp strokes of the park scene.

Adam sighed and put the painting aside. His eyes met hers. "What you saw was a lovely illusion."

She stared at him. "What do you mean?"

"How do you suppose I happen to have a famous painting worth thousands, which has been hanging on the walls of a prominent gallery?"

"I don't know," she stammered. "I didn't think about that."

Inspector Theo Muller spoke up now. "I will clarify it for you, Miss Sheldon. The painting you identified as a Kelzer just now is not authentic. It is a most realistic and falsely aged copy by a talented artist, Adam Bond."

She stared at him. "You did that?"

"Yes," he said. "I've done several like it."

"But that's against the law," she protested.

He shook his head. "Not when they are marked as copies and sold for a reasonable price. Some people collect such replicas of famous paintings."

"But the police have become involved?" she said, baffled.

Inspector Muller nodded. "So they have, Miss Sheldon. Because a criminal gang have been employing good artists down on their luck to make these copies of great paintings and through associates in the various museums have been removing the real masterpieces from their frames in the midnight hours and replacing them with fakes so excellent the substitutions were not discovered for a long time."

"What did they do with the real paintings?" she asked.

"They went on the black market, miss," the inspector said sternly. "There are wealthy, avaricious individuals who want such art even if they dare not display it. And they often pay huge amounts for the paintings. So the grim business flourishes."

She looked at Adam, still bewildered. "But you didn't need to do such a thing. You had that excellent portrait commission of Vivian Lane. Why did you get mixed up in it?"

Adam said, "I was approached by the leader of the ring. His headquarters is in Berlin. That's one reason why I made those hasty trips."

"So you are a criminal, after all," she said.

"Not quite." The inspector smiled. "When Adam was approached by this evil genius, he went straight to the police. To my division, which has to do with frauds and the like. We asked him to join in with the scheme as a favor to us, to infiltrate the gang and get as much information as he could gather. He has done very well indeed."

"As soon as the rest of the gang are arrested, I'm free of it all," Adam told her.

"All the time you were really a decoy working to help the police," she said with relief.

"That's exactly it," Adam said. "I'm glad it's over. I've felt awful, having to deceive you and my other friends. But I felt this was a crime against art and I should help."

"I agree," she said.

"Just a few more hours," the inspector said. "There are some details to be recorded at headquarters. Then we'll trouble Mr. Bond and his friends no more."

"It will be in all the newspapers this afternoon," Adam said. "Maybe your friend Frank will be on it. He's doing a magazine piece."

She nodded. "He told me he had some facts on you but couldn't reveal them because he had a deal with the police."

Inspector Muller smiled. "It will all be out today. I should expect Mr. Bond's name will be in all the headlines. He'll be a sort of a hero!"

Sally groaned. "I know what that will mean!"

"What?" Adam asked.

"Dorothy will really be after you again."

"I thought you said she was all through with me." The young artist smiled.

"She has a weakness for heroes, does Dorothy," Sally told him.

Adam and Inspector Muller took her downtown in a police car and dropped her off at her hotel. She had lunch and then rested a little.

The ugly burden which had been lifted from her made her feel her vacation had been a wonderful success after all.

She knew she had to face calling the Lanes at their hotel. She had promised the old woman she would let her know any news and she made a practice of keeping her word. She well knew that Dorothy would at once do a quick switch and be endorsing Adam again and trying to win him for herself. But she had to take that risk.

She used the phone in the lobby and got through to Vivian Lane almost at once. She quickly told her what she had found out, ending with, "So Adam was never in trouble with the police; he was actually working for them."

"I'm not surprised," the old woman said. "I had more faith in that young man than Dorothy."

Sally asked, "I wonder what she'll say now?"

"Dorothy changes her opinions and moods with the weather," the old woman said. "Since this weather report is fair, I expect she'll be sunny and loving again."

Sally laughed. "Well, at least now you know."

"Did you see my portrait when you were there?" the old woman asked.

"Yes. Carefully covered with a white sheet."

"I'm going to arrange to take delivery of it and we'll have a party for you at the same time," Aunt Vivian said. "We'll do it as soon as we can."

"You mustn't worry about me," Sally said.

"I'm old enough to worry about anyone I want to," was the old woman's reply.

Sally remained close to the hotel all afternoon. Around four, there was a knock on her bedroom door. When she opened it, she saw a smiling Frank standing there with a newspaper in his hands. He handed it to her so she could see the large photo of Adam on the front page.

He quoted the headline: "Artist Foils Art Thefts!" And with a sad smile, he said, "I'm offering you a hero. I guess that's the end of things for me."

She smiled. "Don't be too sure! There's always Dorothy! Heroes are her special interest!"

CHAPTER FIFTEEN

Frank insisted that they celebrate by having dinner that night at the elegant New World Hotel.

After they were seated, Sally whispered across the table, "This must be awfully expensive!"

"It is," he whispered back. "But it goes on the expense account because you'll be giving me your impressions of Adam Bond for a story in tomorrow's paper. I sometimes do newspaper stuff, too."

"That will be easy," she said. "I think he's wonderful."

Frank winced. "I was afraid you'd say something like that."

The menu had a wide range of items, but they were in the mood for steaks American style. So that was what they ordered. Sally was impressed by the fine service and the elegant table settings.

Happily the food proved equally good. And all too soon they had arrived at coffee and an apple dessert. Sally found herself speculating on where Adam might be on this evening of his triumph.

She asked the young writer, "Where do you suppose Adam is tonight?"

"He could still be with the police, cleaning things up," Frank suggested. "A couple of the criminals are still at large."

"Would he be in any danger from them, do you think?"

"You never can be sure," he said. "They'll definitely not be in a good mood. He's exposed their entire setup. It's the end of a nice source of easy money for them."

"I'd like to hear the whole story from him," Sally said."

"No doubt you will."

She smiled at Frank across the table. "You forget I fly back to New York and work in another few days."

The young writer looked upset. "I hadn't realized the time had passed so quickly. Can't you take a few days extra?"

Sally shook her head. "I couldn't afford it and I'm due back at my job. I've had a longer than usual vacation as it is."

His eyes met hers. "Why not stay in Amsterdam?"

She said, "I think I'd miss home."

"We need someone at the PR office. No hard work, just take care of mail and type a few letters," Frank said. "I could get you the job."

"But you'll probably be leaving here soon," she told him. "You never stay in one place for long."

"In another few months I'll likely be going elsewhere," he admitted. "Maybe even back to New York."

"I'll see you then."

He said, "Remember I did make a serious offer. And you have really never given me a proper answer."

"I'm not ready to make any decisions," she said. "Not yet."

"Because of Adam?"

"Partly," she said. "And partly because I want to make sure I have the same feelings when I get back home."

Frank studied her good-humoredly. "I'll say this. You always have some sort of good excuse to offer me."

"I'm fond of you," she said. "I can't imagine us not being friends."

"I have more ambitious plans for us than that," Frank told her.

It was a lovely, warm night when they left the hotel and so they walked back slowly through the clean streets. There was moonlight and they stopped to study its reflection in a distant canal for a while. They both became oddly silent, walking hand in hand, knowing they would soon be parted.

Finally, they came to the busier area where her hotel was located, the small hotel that would always be dear to her heart. She and Frank stood facing each other on the sidewalk, still unable to find the right words.

"I'll miss you," he said at last.

"And I'll miss you," she was quick to say.

He summoned a twisted smile. "Why are we so unhappy? We have some time left here."

She picked up his wry humor. "Hours and hours to spare!" she declared.

"I'll be in touch in the morning," Frank said. "I'm going to try and get a few days off. So we can have extra time before you leave."

"Don't put yourself out for me, please," she said.

"Wouldn't you like me to have the last days with you?"

"Yes, of course," she said. "But I'll be packing and I'll be seeing Dorothy and her aunt. And—"

He nodded. "I know. And our hero, Adam. He's the important one."

"I will want to see him," she said quietly.

"I know," he said. Then he took her in his

arms for a gentle embrace and a brief kiss. "See you tomorrow," he said with another of his wry smiles and moved down the street.

She felt a distinct sadness as she went into the hotel. She had come to depend on Frank a great deal and she would surely miss him. She was so lost in these thoughts that she passed by the familiar figure of Inspector Theo Muller without even noticing him.

The man stepped forward and, bowing, said, "Good evening, Miss Sheldon."

She gasped. "I'm sorry. I was a thousand miles away in my thoughts."

"Quite all right," he said. "I have been waiting here to see you."

"Oh?" She stared into the man's lined face.

He seemed to be having some difficulty finding proper words, for he hesitated a long moment. "I have been concerned about your safety."

"I was out to dinner with a friend," she said. "Why should you be worried about me?"

Inspector Muller frowned. "We did not arrest the last of the art fraud gang until this evening. In the meantime, one of them went on a violent binge."

She felt a tightening at her throat. "Was Adam involved?"

"He was attacked in his studio," the inspector said. "Knocked senseless, and considerable harm was done there."

Her panic increased. "Was he hurt badly?"

"Fortunately not," the inspector said. "But he is remaining in the hospital overnight for observation. At times these head blows can be more dangerous than expected."

"I understand," she said. "Would I be able to see him?"

"I very much doubt it," the inspector said gently. "We were afraid this fellow knew about your friendship with Adam and might have also tried to harm you."

"Nothing happened at all."

"That is good," Inspector Muller said. "We have him safely in custody now. There is no need to be afraid. We have them all."

"How much damage was done at Adam's studio?"

"A good deal," the inspector sighed. "I shall be going there the first thing in the morning to make a listing. You know what he had. You might be able to help. Would you come along?"

"Yes," she said. "Do let me go there with you."

"I will come by at nine," the inspector said.

"I'll be ready," she promised. "Thank you."

He left and the night elevator man took her up to her room. Despite the fact she'd had a long and weary day, she felt little like sleeping. She'd gone about with Frank, blissfully unaware that she might have been in danger. And Adam had been struck down by the vengeful gangster.

And there had been a good deal of damage

at his studio. That worried her a lot. The inspector hadn't said what sort of damage, but she could only hope that most of his paintings had escaped. Especially the huge portrait of Vivian Lane waiting to be delivered.

Sally had another restless night and rose early in the morning to be ready for the inspector when he came by for her. The man arrived in a police car a few minutes before the appointed time, and she was on the sidewalk waiting for him.

As she joined him in the car, she asked, "Have you had any late word on Adam?"

"He is still in the hospital, but they expect to release him sometime this morning or afternoon," the inspector said.

She sighed. "I hardly slept all night."

"I'm sorry I had to break the news to you the way I did," he apologized.

"It was the only way," she said. "I was going to tell some other American friends of Adam's, but I decided to wait. He has done a fine portrait of one of them. He was just about to deliver it. It's important to him since it means a large fee. I didn't dare to phone them until I saw that the portrait wasn't damaged."

The inspector said, "I can't tell you about that. But we'll be there in a few minutes. We've kept an officer on the premises all night."

They reached the building where the studio was located and she had a peculiar feeling as she walked into the big room with the inspector. As she took stock of things, her stomach became queasy. Almost all the pictures on the walls, including hers, had been splashed with paints and ruined.

"So much vandalism!" she murmured.

"Very little left intact," the inspector agreed.

She approached the large painting and was relieved to see that it was still covered with its white sheet. Her hand trembling just a little, she lifted the sheet, and the slashed, mutilated canvas made her moan.

"Ruined!" she lamented. "The lovely portrait ruined!"

"I saw it before," the inspector said. "It was a magnificent piece of work."

"It represented weeks of hard work, months!" Sally said. "All lost."

The inspector looked grim. "We did not expect the violence nor the vandalism. We should have taken precautions."

"Well, too late now," she said bleakly.

"A pity," the inspector sighed.

He went on taking stock of the damage. She sat down near Adam's phone and put a call through to the Lanes. It was Dorothy who answered the phone. And as soon as she recognized Sally's voice, she showed a much changed mood.

"Isn't it thrilling?" she exclaimed. "Adam is a hero!"

"I never did think he'd done anything much wrong," Sally told her.

"Nor I," said the girl on the other end of the line, conveniently forgetting all she'd said earlier.

"There's more to the story," Sally went on. "Adam was attacked in his studio and a lot of damage was done here. He's in the hospital, but he's expected out today."

Dorothy became distraught. "He's not badly hurt?"

"They don't think so."

"Then it's all right," Dorothy said, seeming relieved. "After all we've gone through, I don't think I could bear that."

"Most of his paintings were destroyed by the man who attacked him," Sally said. "Including mine and yours."

"What about Aunt Vivian's portrait?" Dorothy asked.

"Destroyed," she said in a small voice. "Utterly ruined."

There was a silence at the other end of the line. Then Dorothy said, "I'll tell Aunt Vivian. Perhaps it can be repaired."

"I've examined it," Sally said. "He'd have to do it over again."

"I see," Dorothy said. "Tell Adam I want to see him as soon as possible."

"I will," she said listlessly.

"You'll be leaving in a day or two, won't you?" Dorothy added.

"Day after tomorrow."

"Well, Amsterdam will miss you," Dorothy

said without too much enthusiasm. "You'll not forget winning that contest for a long while."

"I'll remember all my life," Sally assured her.

"We must try and get together before you go," Dorothy said. "And if we miss each other, we must keep in touch by mail."

"I'll remember that," she said, knowing full well the flighty Dorothy would never write a line.

She hung up the phone and sat there sadly for a while as the inspector went on making notes about the damage. Then she went and picked up the portrait of herself that Adam had done from memory. A dab of scarlet paint had been savagely slashed across the middle of her face. She studied the mutilated portrait with sad eyes.

Then she heard footsteps coming up the stairway. She dropped the portrait and moved toward the door just in time to meet Adam. He had a white bandage around his head and looked terribly pale. He saw her and came to her and took her in his arms.

"Sally!" he said with emotion.

"Adam!" She nestled happily in his arms. "Are you all right?"

"Yes, fine," he said. "I'll have the bandage off in a day or so." Then he let her go as he prepared to move further into the studio.

She held on to his arm, pleading, "Don't worry! It will be all right!"

But he had already seen enough to make him understand the full extent of the damage. He moved forward like someone in a dream, holding up one piece of ruined work and allowing it to fall from his fingers, moving on and picking up another, and doing the same thing with it.

At last he came to the portrait of Vivian Lane. He lifted the protective sheet and stared at the mutilation, his handsome face blank of expression. Then he let the sheet drop and turned and rushed past Sally out of the studio and down the stairway.

Sally turned desperately to the inspector. "What can we do? Someone should go with him!"

"I think not," the inspector said. "He must adjust to this in his own way. I'm sure he will. But we both know what a bad blow it has been."

"So unfair," she said, tears in her eyes. "So very unfair."

The inspector patted her gently on the arm. "At least you were here to greet him. He'll remember that when he's able to get his thoughts straight again."

"You think so?" she worried.

"I'm certain of it," he said. "He is a brave man and a strong one or he would not have gone through the risk he did. He will recover from this."

She had no more word from Adam that day

or night. Luckily Frank was around to keep her company whenever he was needed. She had him take her back to the studio, but it was locked and the place dark. So she assumed Adam had not returned there.

As they got back in Frank's rented car, she asked, "Where do you think he has gone?"

"I couldn't guess," the writer said. "I know how he must feel."

"I'm worried for him," she said.

"Don't be," Frank told her. "Give him a little time and he'll be back at your hotel proposing to you again!"

She smiled through her concern. "I hardly think he has his mind on anything like that at the moment."

"You might be surprised," the writer said. "I predict you'll see or hear from him tomorrow."

"I'd better had," she said. "I'll be leaving the next day."

"He should know that."

"Well," she sighed, "I guess there's nothing to do but wait."

And so she waited. The following morning she was called down to take a message at the desk phone. When she answered, Adam was on the line.

"Sorry to bring you all the way downstairs," he apologized.

"Don't be!" she said, suddenly bursting with happiness. "It's so good to hear from you."

"I'm fine," he said quietly. "Bruised but on the way to recovery. I'm sorry I left you so abruptly yesterday."

"It was all right," she told him.

"Thanks," he said. "You're leaving tomorrow, aren't you?"

"Yes," she agreed. "Not long now."

"There's a party being held for you."

"A party?"

"Yes. Dorothy reached me here at the studio. Her Aunt Vivian is having a farewell party for you in her suite this evening. Frank Kincaid is invited and so am I."

She was taken completely by surprise at first, then remembered Aunt Vivian had mentioned a party at one point.

"Vivian Lane is quite a gal," Adam said. "You will be receiving a formal invitation by messenger, but she gave me the privilege of telling you. Be at her suite at seven."

"What about you?"

"I'll meet you there," he said. "I'm busy cleaning up things here or I'd see you before. You know how it is."

"I know," she said sadly. "Then we'll all meet tonight at seven."

She left the phone in a mixed state of mind. She was most grateful to Vivian Lane for holding the party, but there were so many loose ends still unresolved. And that bothered her.

The elaborate invitation, handwritten on the Hotel Grand stationery, arrived later in the day. Sally showed it to Frank and he was pleased at the turn of events.

He said, "My lucky day! Dorothy has her claws in Adam after all."

Sally wore her favorite silk dress. Frank looked very elegant in a well-tailored dark-blue suit. When they arrived at the suite, they found it decorated with flowers.

Vivian Lane, eyes twinkling, came forward to greet them personally. The old woman kissed Sally and said, "You look splendid, my dear!"

Then she led them into the big sitting room where Adam and Dorothy were waiting. Dorothy looked unusually smug in a low-cut gold dress, while Adam had changed from bandage to a band aid at his temple and looked much more like himself.

Vivian Lane stood in the middle of the room and, in regal tones, said, "This is a most special occasion. First, it marks my giving Adam my check for the painting which he is going to do of me when he returns to New York."

Everyone applauded and congratulated Adam, who stood by, looking rather sheepish with Dorothy holding onto his arm and looking up at him with doe eyes.

Vivian Lane cleared her throat. "And secondly, this is a farewell party in honor of someone who has become dear to all of us." She paused for a moment, and it was Sally's turn to blush as the others offered their applause.

Then the old woman continued, "May I say

she is particularly dear to one of us, so much so that he has asked her to be his wife and tonight will give her the engagement ring to seal the bargain."

Sally stood there lost! Her head was in a whirl! She could not believe what she'd heard. Then she saw Adam coming toward her holding a ring in his hand. Dorothy stood back a distance, applauding with the others.

Adam smiled at her and said, "I think that time I asked you, you said yes. But if you didn't, will you say it now?"

Her eyes were blurred with tears of happiness as she looked up at him and said, "I'll say it again for good luck! Yes!"

Adam slipped the ring on her finger and took her in his arms.